Don't meddle in our Romcom, please.

PRASANNA S. NIRANTARE

INDIA • SINGAPORE • MALAYSIA

ISBN

Hardcase 979-8-89906-552-1
Paperback 979-8-89724-273-3

Contents

The Interwoven Stories

Don't Meddle in our Romcom, Please.

The Romcom Plot

"This is the day when it will finally happen," Adi thought to himself nervously as he got ready, checked, and double-checked the contents of his pocket before leaving home.

The sun began to dip below the horizon, casting a warm glow over the lakeside setting. Natalie walked hand in hand with Adi along the picturesque walkway on the cliff overlooking the lake below on the hiking trail.

They had planned an evening excursion along the lake, an hour's drive from Berlin. Natalie would have preferred it in the morning, but Adi insisted on going there in the evening.

Natalie had a familiar smile on her lips. Adi seemed a bit nervous, which gave her an idea that this day would bring something special.

"Adi," she said, breaking the peaceful silence, "you know, you've got one shot at this. I want it to be done properly this time."

Adi chuckled nervously, scratching his head. "Well, I was actually planning something..."

Natalie raised an eyebrow, "Planning something?"

He nodded, "Yeah, something special for you."

Natalie grinned, "You do know I won't say yes unless it's romantic, right? You already tried the unromantic version last time."

Adi blushed, remembering his failed attempt. The memory of the failed attempt clouded his mind. His thoughts drifted to the heartbreak, bringing sudden pain and sorrow. "Let's call it quits."

"Adi. Adi. Where are you lost?"

Natalie touched Adi's shoulder, which brought him back to the present.

"Adi, it had better be good this time," Natalie interrupted his thoughts.

"Ok. This time, it will be romantic. It's sad that in today's world, show and bling have more value than real heartfelt love," Adi teased Natalie.

"Yes, it has." Both laughed as they continued to walk hand in hand.

The sun was about to set as they reached a beautiful clearing in the forest by the lake. It painted the sky in shades of pink and gold. The air was filled with the fragrance of blooming flowers from the trees that covered the forest hiking trail.

Natalie loved the sunsets, and it was the perfect spot.

Earlier that week, Adi had visited the exact spot and waited a full evening to time the sunset.

Natalie couldn't help but feel the excitement bubbling inside her.

"Alright, Adi," she teased, "let's see what you've got."

Taking a deep breath, Adi faced Natalie, his eyes filled with sincerity. "Natalie, from the moment we met, I knew you were the one. You make my every day brighter, my every moment special. I can't imagine my life without you. I love you more than words can convey."

Natalie's heart skipped a beat as she realized this was it—the moment she had been waiting for. She stood there facing Adi as he reached into his pocket to pull out the ring. Seeing this, Natalie's eyes widened, her lips parting in sheer surprise. Overwhelmed by the moment, she instinctively covered her mouth with both hands. A burst of excitement surged through her, and she began to bounce gently on the balls of her feet, the anticipation and joy manifesting in a rhythmic, elated dance.

The elation was short-lived. Adi fumbled and dropped the ring box. The ring parted from the box, rolled gently, and fell across the lake fence into the lake 20 feet below. Adi and Natalie watched this happen in disbelief.

Adi woke up with a start, perspiring heavily.

Smart and the Feisty One

Technology has changed how people see the world, or rather, more precisely, what people can see.

On the other side of the screen, there was Natalie Schmidt. Technology enabled Dr. Revathi Iyengar Sodhi to observe her actions and listen to her words from a distance of 6000 kilometers at that very moment. Revathi watched her every morning as Natalie eloquently narrated the events around the globe, sitting in the studio of DE Media in Berlin.

It could seem usual to most people, but Revathi found this very amusing—the wonder of technology; sitting in her living room sipping hot coffee, she could watch this beautiful girl thousands of kilometers away.

"It's amazing. I can see and listen to this girl, Natalie, right now from here, as she sits and talks from Berlin," she would often exclaim to Harpreet while sipping the morning coffee.

"And the count increases to 536. That's what I was wondering. How come you have not said this today?" Harpreet teased her as they sat in front of the television for the morning coffee, the relaxed 30 minutes of the day before they started the daily grind.

Revathi loved to learn about people and cultures around the world. Hence, foreign news channels on television appealed to her. She used to watch several foreign networks, including news from countries like Russia, Germany, France, and Japan. She was fortunate that these days, most countries relay their English channels despite English not being their native language.

"News channels instead of fiction help us know a real perspective on life from diverse cultures and people."

Recently, she got interested in the German news channel, DE Media, as her son moved to Germany for a new promising job opportunity. Natalie hosted a news show on DE Media from Berlin. Revathi liked Natalie's news show and the way she presented the show. Having married young and become parents soon after, Revathi and Harpreet were in the prime of their careers, even though they now had a grown-up son.

While watching the news show, Revathi observed Natalie's dresses and jewelry and read her expressions. Revathi enjoyed using her skills to understand people and imagine what their lives might be like. Doing so for someone on television thousands of miles away made it more fun.

Revathi was a psychology professor and a practitioner. She had a doctorate in psychology, and years of practice had made her an expert in human behavior and psychology. This understanding gave her the power to read people's minds through facial expressions. She seemed to possess extraordinary abilities, much like the special powers of a

Marvel superhero. Special power of face reading and reading people's minds. With this special power, along with a deep understanding of human psychology, she could influence anyone to act as per her will.

"She looks quite bubbly today. It seems she has got some good news."

"You got all that from her face, right?" Even after so many years of witnessing Revathi's expertise, Harpreet found it unreal and amusing.

Revathi used to oversimplify things and would often say, "Face reading is not magic or some superpower. With a little understanding of human psychology, keen observation, and the skill of deduction, anyone can read a person like an open book."

For the less aware, she would explain further, going into more depth. "Humans can produce a wide range of facial expressions, which are typically composed of movements of the face muscles, lips, mouth, forehead, cheeks, eyes, and even eyebrows. Combinations of these movements can create numerous expressions, and each expression conveys a different emotion and state of a person's mind. Eyes give away the most."

Harpreet had heard all of it many times. Revathi decided to spare him the whole explanation. She kept it short.

"Eyes can talk, you know."

"Yes. I know it very well. I am left with no thoughts that are private, just mine. I feel mentally naked in front of you," Harpreet flirted.

"Yes, mentally or physically, I can undress you at my will," Revathi flirted back. Revathi and Harpreet had been married for 30 years. The spark was still alive and flaring between them.

Back in the day, Revathi and Harpreet's love story was the talk of their university, if not the whole town. Revathi was an outgoing, smart, extroverted girl, unlike the stereotypical timid and shy image that a Tamil Brahmin girl had. An image that movies typically portray of a heroine from that background. At 5'7", she was considered tall compared to an average Indian girl. She had a slender build and erect posture. Revathi put a small black bindi on her forehead, which, by his own confession, stole Harpreet's heart. The small black bindi, which started as a tradition in her childhood, stuck on as a fashion statement in her youth. The bindi still adorned her forehead out of habit. Harpreet's affection for that look with the bindi made him lose his heart to Revathi in college. He was still a fan of that look.

Harpreet was a shy, introverted boy, contrasting sharply with the outgoing, tall, and well-built image typically associated with Punjabi boys, especially as popularized in films. Despite being well-built, he stood at only 5'9".

They met at the university, where Harpreet studied finance while Revathi pursued psychology. Punjabis and Tamils are poles apart, geographically and culturally. Generally, they do not have too much respect for each other. That did not stop Harpreet and Revathi from falling in love. However, their families did not share the same love and respect for each other, and their families did not agree to their wedding.

The day both Revathi and Harpreet secured jobs and hence were no longer dependent on their families, Revathi took the driver's seat on the matter. She wrote a letter to both their families, which in the literal sense was the opposite of the phrase--*beating around the bush.*

Dear Parents,

We are getting married. That is final.

We understand that your dislike of each other stems from the cultural differences between the Punjabi and Tamil communities. We understand that it is difficult for you. However, you have only two choices.

1. *Either accept our marriage and both families meet occasionally for festivals and events, tolerate each other, and everyone lives their life happily.*
2. *Do not accept our marriage; everyone lives their life with grudge and sadness.*

If I were you, I would choose happiness over sadness any day. Please let us know your choice.

Also, we will have kids someday, and you will not get to meet your grandkids if you choose option 2.

Yours lovingly,
Revathi and Harpreet

Their parents had no choice but to pick option 1.

Revathi and Harpreet got married soon after. It wasn't long before they were blessed with Adi when Revathi and Harpreet were only 22 and 25 years old, respectively. Revathi further completed her master's degree and PhD in psychology after she had Adi.

And They Met

Adi declined the invitation for hiking on Saturday morning, much to the disappointment of the person on the other end of the line.

"Spend time with your wife and kids. When I visited your place for dinner last week, she complained to me that you spent too much time…wait, what was the word she used… Yes, you spend too much time loitering around with me." Adi hung up the phone.

Adi did not care what his wife thought, but it was an excuse to get out of the Saturday morning hiking proposal. He wanted to spend a laid-back, relaxed Saturday morning.

Adi had a laid-back, relaxed personality. He lived life at his own pace, not getting pulled into the rush of his surroundings and the world. He lived with the belief and debated wherever possible that if the whole world slowed down and took a pause, it would be a much happier place. It was his belief; however, the world did not move as per his belief. Though he had a laid-back attitude, he had good determination. Once he decided to do something, he would put 100% into achieving it. He wasn't too ambitious, but he knew what he needed to do to be successful in life.

At 5'11" and lean-built, he was a handsome young man. He was born to middle-class parents in a family that believed education was the key to success, reinforcing the importance of studies from a young age. He was an introvert and spoke only when necessary. An extension of this quality was his involuntary trait, which he could not overcome even if he tried to. He shared information only when necessary or asked for.

Since childhood, Adi burdened himself with the idea of "Do what you say." It was wired in his brain. The side effect of this was he delayed decisions and unless sure, he would not say or commit to anything. He would even avoid situations that would lead people to believe something he is not sure of fulfilling. This quality of his would turn his world upside down at some point in his life.

The next day, Adi spent a relaxed Saturday morning that started with a morning tea with the newspaper and then some television. Later, he spent almost an hour chatting on his phone. Emotions that the word "typing" on the chat window invokes vary depending on the current phase of the relationship. It brought Adi immense relief to see *typing* when he first messaged her, unsure if she would respond. After that, every time he replied, *typing* brought a feeling of excitement and anticipation of the reply that he would get.

How about dinner tonight?

The chat window read *typing* at the top below her name. He was eagerly waiting for the response when the phone rang.

It was Revathi. Adi was not happy with the timing of the call as he was eagerly waiting for the reply in the chat.

"Hi, Amma, good morning. No, good afternoon."

"Good morning, Adi. How are you? I thought I would call now as we are going out later."

"Sure, Ma," Adi was still lost, eagerly waiting for the message.

Sure. I am in for dinner.

I will text you the location. See you then, Adi replied.

"Are you busy? You seem lost. We can talk later," his mother asked.

"No, no, it's fine." Adi was happy about the confirmed dinner date, and that was reflected on his face. Revathi noticed the change in his expression and realized something was going on.

"What news?" she probed.

"Nothing much, just routine."

Revathi knew there was something, but she decided not to probe further. Her family had learned over the years that Revathi was too good at what she did: psychology and face reading. She could read all of them like an open book. However, Revathi had learned over the years, too, not to use her skills with family and to let things be as normal as possible. She would let Adi be until he told her, even if she read that something was up with him.

Revathi's day started with Natalie from Berlin in the morning, and her day ended with a video call with her son in Berlin. However, the end-of-the-day routine was once or twice a week, not a daily ritual. She would love everyday calls, but it was too much for Adi. Her motherly questions about food, clothing for cold weather, and general well-being advice would get too boring for him.

"Yes, Mum, I am eating fruits and veggies and drinking milk, and I do put on warm clothes, and I don't stay up too late at night, and I take care of myself, and I will call you."

Adi would say this even before Revathi started with her motherly advice. Both would have a good laugh at this. With the routine question-and-answer out of the way, they would move on to talk about other topics. They liked to talk about current affairs, politics, cooking, food, relatives, friends, and more.

"How can someone talk for an hour on the phone?" Harpreet used to comment. He was old school and used the phone only to convey messages to the point. His calls wouldn't last more than five minutes.

One week ago, Adi's Saturday was very different. He had some deadlines to meet at work, so he was in the office on a Saturday.

"Who goes to work on a Saturday? No one, right? You don't work on a Saturday, right? But I have to. Forget it, I am not going tomorrow. I will see what happens on Monday," Adi had cribbed about it to his buddy on a Friday night.

Yet, there he was in the office on a Saturday morning, sacrificing his much-cherished laid-back Saturday morning. He reached the office at 7 a.m., earlier than usual. His office was on Kurfürstendamm—the vibrant, bustling street known for its high-end shops, restaurants, and corporate offices in Berlin. Adi was hoping to finish his work before lunch so that he would get the rest of his weekend free. He had underestimated the complexity of the task at hand. As he started digging into the problem, it unraveled multiple layers of complexity. It was lunchtime, and he was still nowhere close to completion. Frustrated and hungry, Adi decided to push through and finish before going for lunch. It was 3:10 p.m. by the time he was done. As he was shutting down his laptop, he saw a severe weather warning alert on his taskbar.

Very heavy rain and thunderstorms.

Hungry, he decided to go to the café nearby to grab some food.

The café was partially crowded; only a couple of tables were occupied. There was an elderly couple sitting at a table in the corner and a young girl sitting at the tall table along the outside glass façade of the café. She had a book in her hand and occasionally watched the world go by on the outside pavement and the street beyond it. The television, mounted high and suspended from the ceiling, played the same severe weather warning on the weather channel. Adi had noticed the girl at the tall table as he walked inside the café. He found her beautiful, attractive, and familiar. It was Natalie Schmidt.

Natalie was a young woman with brown hair and hazel eyes, 5'7" tall, slender, and beautiful. Natalie was born and raised in a small town called Lüneburg, known for its charming medieval architecture, picturesque streets, and rich history. It is about a two-hour train ride from Berlin. Natalie was raised by very loving parents, Bernhard and Marie. Natalie graduated in mass communication and worked very hard to reach the position she holds today. Right from her childhood, she was a principled and idealistic girl. There were several instances where she found herself in a tough spot due to this, but she did not let go of her principles. Once, during her graduate studies, she noticed that a professor unfairly treated a fellow student. Passionate about fighting for a social cause, she courageously stood by her classmate to ensure that justice was served despite the potential backlash.

This nature helped her excel in her profession in journalism and media.

The dark clouds had gathered in the sky, making the atmosphere dull and dark outside, as if it would start pouring any second.

Adi placed his order at the counter before approaching Natalie.

"Excuse me, are you Natalie Schmidt? The famous TV star?"

Natalie laughed, "Yes, it's me, but I am hardly a television star."

Natalie found Adi's comment flattering.

"Do I know you?"

"I suppose not, but I've seen you on TV countless times. Your reporting is always so captivating."

"Oh, thank you! It's always nice to meet a viewer. What brings you here today?"

"I am Adi. I work nearby, round the corner. I am here to grab a late lunch. Can I buy you a coffee to show my appreciation for your work?"

Natalie found Adi's personality pleasing.

"That's very kind of you, Adi. I'd like that. Thank you."

Adi sat down at the same table as Natalie.

"So, what's it like being a well-known face on TV? It must come with its own set of challenges."

"It's been a journey. Balancing professionalism with the public's expectations can be tricky. But I'm grateful for the platform that TV provides me to engage with the people."

"I can imagine. You always seem so composed and articulate on screen. Especially that one piece you did on the drug problem in Germany. That was very intense. How do you handle the pressure?" Natalie was impressed that Adi wasn't just flattering her; he actually followed her work.

There was a call from the counter for the ordered food and coffee. Adi promptly went and brought the tray to the table.

Adi was very hungry and couldn't wait. As he sat down with his food, he forgot about Natalie and hastily ate his food from the plate. Natalie smiled as she watched Adi eat hastily.

"Someone seems very hungry."

"Yes," Adi gave an awkward smile. "Sorry, I was too hungry. Now I am better."

"They say if you want to know anyone's true nature, observe them when they are very hungry."

"Is it? And what did you get to know about me?"

"The composure and depth of the conversation while you were so hungry. Not bad, I would say. Not bad." They laughed.

Both engaged in a thoughtful and engaging discussion on various topics. Adi wasn't afraid to express his own views on different topics that didn't exactly align with celebrity TV host Natalie's views. Natalie was impressed by Adi's awareness, intelligence, and independent thinking.

As Adi finished his food, it started raining heavily. The visibility outside the window seemed nil.

"Looks like we will be here for a while. Would you like another coffee?"

"Sure. But the coffee for my appreciation as a TV host is done. This one, I will pay."

"Okay. Suit yourself. Will you pay for mine, too?"

"Okay. If you insist." They laughed again.

This conversation triggered a thought in Adi's mind that he could not resist discussing with Natalie.

"You know what, this modern trend of girls wanting to pay for their order is a little off-putting."

"Interesting. How so?" Natalie was almost offended and a little disappointed by Adi's statement, but she did not want to be judgmental and jump to conclusions in haste.

"I will explain. Imagine you are on a date, and the girl says we will split the bill 50-50. It takes the romance out of the date. It takes away the role of a provider from the boy." Natalie was even more disappointed by Adi's explanation. It was starting to irritate her.

"Provider. Now, who gave that role to a man? It's an age-old role definition and the root cause of all women's exploitation," Natalie was dead serious when she delivered that sentence. Adi realized he was treading on thin ice talking about this topic, but the topic was too interesting and what he believed in to let go of now.

Adi did not react instantly. He took a pause, smiled, and then spoke.

"Hear me out. There is a certain romance in a boy paying for a date. Splitting the bill makes it very transactional. How can love bloom in such a transactional environment?"

"But this provider mindset builds and supports the notion that women take care of the home, do cleaning, washing, cooking, take care of kids while men sit there on the sofa watching television."

"Okay, if a girl feels that way, then she should pay. I am fine with that, too. But this 50:50 thing is very unromantic. It kills emotional bonding."

"No. Why should girls pay?"

"So that she can be the provider."

Adi laughed, thinking he had cracked a great joke. Natalie stared at him with a frown, almost annoyed.

"Sorry. Sorry. I didn't mean it like that. I think that was a bad joke."

With a nervous, concerned look on his face, he tried to recover from the mess.

There was a long pause as Adi sat there looking at his coffee, thinking about what to say next. Natalie found it cute—the way Adi was nervously sitting there like a small child in front of a teacher after making a mistake. Natalie was surprised with herself. Typically, she would have had an argument in such a situation.

It continued raining heavily, and the café was almost empty. The girl at the counter was busy staring at her phone, while the elderly couple in the corner silently stared outside the window, probably contemplating when the weather would get better. In the silence, the TV sound came to the fore, playing in the background while they were conversing. Natalie decided to relieve Adi from his agony.

"Yes. It was a bad joke. You seem to have that habit of making the wrong joke on the wrong topic," Natalie smiled, relieving him from his agony.

Adi used to enjoy a good debate and wished to continue the discussion with Natalie. But he trod more carefully this time.

"Please don't mind, but may I ask you something?"

"Go ahead."

"According to you, what should be the roles of man and woman in a relationship?" Natalie had not given this a thought, but the question was deep and made her think. After a moment's pause, she replied.

"Men and women should have equal roles and responsibilities in a relationship."

"I agree with you on that. But do you think it is that simple?"

"What do you mean?"

"Every individual is different, and their needs from a relationship are different. So instead of pursuing equality, one should pursue meeting each other's needs in a relationship."

Natalie did not agree with everything Adi said, but his thoughts intrigued her. She was impressed by his capacity to think independently about a sensitive subject with such ease, especially in front of her, who had such strong views on feminism.

"For example, what if a girl wants to be a homemaker and take care of her family? She doesn't want to have an equal professional career like her boyfriend or husband."

"Well, then, she should have the liberty to do that."

"She will be lucky if it is that simple. But usually it is not."

"Go on."

"Let's say this couple in question is struggling financially, and a little earning from the wife would go a long way. Is it wrong for the husband to expect her to work?"

Natalie disagreed with the logic.

"The final choice is still hers. It also depends on whether the husband is doing enough or is a good-for-nothing drunkard. Also, will he help her with household chores if she decides to work?"

"Exactly, it is not simple and depends on multiple factors."

"I agree."

Adi felt happy seeing Natalie agreeing to his thoughts. It encouraged him to continue.

"Well, another situation, though rare, could be that a husband wants to be a stay-at-home husband. Will he get the same freedom of choice we were talking about for the wife? A man typically will not be given a choice. It's like…"

Natalie slipped into an animated voice. "BE A MAN. THE PROVIDER. It's your responsibility to provide for the family."

Both laughed.

Hearing this, Adi looked visibly glad and impressed by Natalie's open and unbiased thinking.

"I am glad you brought that up. I had this in mind, but I was scared to bring it up as it sounded a little anti-feminist."

Natalie burst into laughter. "Scared of me. Am I that devilish?"

Both laughed again.

As the debate in the café warmed up, the thunder roared louder, and the rain poured more heavily.

"Good discussion. We can conclude there is no one right answer."

"The motto should be to put each other's needs first for the relationship to win."

The collective wisdom on relationships that Natalie and Adi discussed in that café was so rich that if they were a couple and lived by this wisdom, their relationship would flourish, and they would never fight. However, theories seldom work in real life. Challenges crop up when couples do not personalize this wisdom before applying it to their relationship. Each couple is different; each situation is different.

It had stopped raining, and the elderly couple left.

"Trapped at the café. Time well spent. Thank you for the wonderful time, Natalie."

"I had a wonderful time as well. Please get the bill. I don't want to take the romance out of this date by going 50-50," Natalie coyly smiled.

The First Fight

Over the next few days, Revathi noticed a twinkle in Adi's eyes and general enthusiasm and happiness in Adi's voice and conversations. She tried to figure it out by asking, "What's new?" The enquiry was responded to with a standard answer.

"Nothing much. Just routine."

Revathi could see something was going on with him, so she decided to wait and observe. Around the same time, Revathi also observed changes in Natalie's demeanor on her television show. Natalie seemed more cheerful in her facial expressions, voice modulation, and tone.

"It could not be a coincidence. Adi is happy, and Natalie also seems to have a sudden twinkle in her eyes."

"Revathi, you are reading too much into it," Harpreet opposed Revathi's speculations.

"Think. Both are in Berlin. Both are showing positive changes in facial expressions and behavior."

"There is no denying. Your face reading and psychology skills are the best. But linking them is just too far-fetched."

It was a typical morning at the Revathi-Harpreet house. Revathi was parked in front of the television, watching the news with a coffee mug in her hand. Harpreet parked himself next to her, screening the newspaper. Morning coffee was Harpreet's job. The doorbell rang. It was Mala, the housemaid. Baban, her husband, had accompanied Mala that day, as Revathi had called him. Baban was the local ironman. Baban ran a local laundry in the basement parking of the city apartment. He used to collect the clothes, iron them, and deliver them back. Mala and Baban were natives of a small fishing village in Konkan, a coastal belt in the state of Maharashtra in western India. They dreamed of owning a fishing boat in their village, but life had other plans. Unable to save enough to own a boat and struggling to make ends meet, they took up an opportunity to move to the city. They have been living in Mumbai since then and made Mumbai their home. They are happy in the small world they've created for themselves in Mumbai.

"Mr. Ironman, have a cup of coffee before you go. Mala, make one for Baban as well."

"No, sir. Let him go. He is very lazy. He will not finish today's clothes delivery. He just needs a reason to waste time."

"See, she started again. I tell you, Madam, I do not get even one moment of peace with her. She is always after me," Baban hesitated and stopped as Mala gave a stern look.

"Just one coffee; it will take 10 minutes."

Baban sat on a chair near the door.

"How is Adi, Sir?"

"He is doing well. You know, he is in Berlin, in Germany, right?"

"Madam, get him married now. How many years will he stay alone like this?"

Revathi flipped the television channel to German DE Media as she replied.

"Yes, why not. But we should find someone that he likes first. That too in Germany."

Hello. Good morning, everyone. This is Natalie Schmidt live from Berlin.

Baban understood a little bit of English and picked up this line from television.

"See. She is from Berlin. She is so pretty. They will make a beautiful couple," Baban sounded sincere in his remark.

"Wow! Mr. Ironman has quite an imagination for romance. I hear you have an interesting love story of your own. I would like to hear that someday."

"Sure, Sir. Whenever you say. Mine and my Mala's love story…" Baban almost blushed while Mala got angry.

"Okay, enough. Have this coffee quickly and get back to your work," Mala said, stopping Baban from having unnecessary conversations.

Revathi was quiet. The comment from Baban sparked a stream of wishful thinking in Revathi's mind.

That night, Revathi shared her wishful thinking with Harpreet.

"Natalie is so beautiful and smart. She is like a celebrity. She will be such a nice bride for Adi. Imagine a German daughter-in-law," she was smiling, lost in imagination.

"Revathi Madam, enough. Please come out of the dreamland," Harpreet responded.

Adi and Natalie's love was gradually blossoming. Dinner dates progressed into movie dates, weekend picnics at a park, shopping outings, etc. They connected very well and became very fond of each other. This showed up in their expressions and voices.

A month had passed since the initial signs she saw in Adi and Natalie's expressions. However, since then, she had noticed nothing additional to back Revathi's hypothesis. She was getting impatient.

"I told you. It was a coincidence."

Driven by her wishful thinking, Revathi was not convinced.

"I know those expressions. I am convinced it was not a coincidence."

"Reach out to Sameer and Malini. They would know."

"No. It's too early for that."

"So, you are having doubts; it might just be unreal wishful thinking on your part."

"No, I am sure about this. I know it. But I don't want to talk to Malini yet."

It was Friday evening, and Natalie was seated alone in a cinema theater next to a vacant seat. The loud sound of the previews could not soothe the tide of disappointment that Natalie was feeling for Adi.

Adi and Natalie had planned for a movie night out. They had planned to meet at the cinema theater after work, 30 minutes before the movie. Natalie finished her work on time and reached the theater as planned. Adi wasn't there. Adi was stuck in a meeting at his office, which had extended beyond his expectations. Being in the middle of a serious discussion, Adi could neither call nor message Natalie about him getting delayed. After waiting for 10 minutes, Natalie called Adi. Adi had his phone on silent mode for the meeting and he did not respond. Natalie tried multiple times after that, but she got no response.

As soon as the meeting concluded, Adi saw several missed calls from Natalie and called her back. Natalie was already annoyed and angry at Adi for such irresponsible behavior and for not meeting his commitment. Adi called her, apologized, and promised to be there at the earliest. He arrived an hour late.

"I am sorry. I got stuck in a meeting."

"It's Ok."

Adi knew it was not okay. Both saw the movie in silence.

After the movie at dinner, Natalie was still in a foul mood because Adi was late. She got more annoyed at Adi's casual apology for the mistake he made, as if nothing had happened. Adi was on a different page altogether. Adi failed to understand what the big deal was. Adi felt that Natalie should understand that he didn't do it on purpose and that he was genuinely stuck in a meeting. She should not make a big issue out of it.

They ended up arguing.

On Saturday morning, Revathi had her routine call with her son. He looked disturbed and angry. He tried to hide his expressions by putting on a fake smile, but in vain. Revathi figured something was bothering Adi. His mind was not in the call and maybe his heart too. Adi seemed preoccupied with his own thoughts. The call was much shorter than usual, and he excused himself with some lame excuse. Revathi, being a mother, wondered what could be troubling her son. She recollected her morning observation of Natalie. Natalie, too, looked lost on the morning show. Being a professional TV presenter, her presentation was flawless, but Revathi had noticed a certain sadness in her eyes and a lack of spark in her expressions.

Revathi was sure this was more than a coincidence. She was fully confident now that Adi and Natalie were a couple.

"Well, you have a point. I cannot deny it," Harpreet also hesitatingly agreed.

"But it is all still circumstantial evidence. We can't prove anything for sure," Harpreet said. He was a courtroom drama buff, which was reflected in his comments.

Over the next few days, Natalie donned a resolute expression on TV, and her son, too, was not himself on the calls. Revathi couldn't stay aloof but meddle. She professionally understood the psychology of people, not excluding that of the young lovers and the petty ups and downs they go through. More recently, her research has been focused on younger demography and their relationships in the modern era. She understood how many love stories that could potentially last for life end due to stupid misunderstandings between young lovers. She often said, "If only these couples had someone to guide them in such times, there would be so little heartbreak in this world."

During her next call with Adi, she pretended to have a big fight with her husband. Adi tried to find out the reason for the fight, to which Revathi just replied, "Ask your father."

Not knowing what the matter was, he called his dad. Harpreet was clueless as to why Revathi was making him do this. He had tried to enquire about the reason, to which she gave her mysterious smile and spoke.

"You will thank me later. It's for the well-being of our son."

Physics and technology interested Harpreet, but when it came to social relationships, emotions, psychology, and matters of love, he left them to his expert wife. It had worked well for the past 28 years since their marriage. He did not intend to change it now. When Adi called, as instructed by Revathi, Harpreet pretended to be in a fight with Revathi. Harpreet narrated the reason for the fight exactly as scripted by Revathi on a piece of paper. Adi was surprised because it was unlike Harpreet to fight over petty matters. Listening to the petty cause of the fight and unnecessary ego on both their parts, Adi tried to reason with his dad, but to no avail. Adi had seen his parents fight before, but they would resolve it among themselves; this was the first time he was pulled into his parents' fight, and that too over a petty matter. He was unsure what changed this time, more so because the matter was so petty.

"Dad, just let go for Mom's sake. You will not become a small person if you give your way for Mom's sake. Let go of your ego," Adi tried to explain to his father. The conversation with his father went on for a while; however, he did not achieve much in the direction of ending his parents' pretend fight. In an attempt to explain to his father, Adi learned an important lesson for himself.

"Winning and being right is not important with loved ones. Ending a fight and making up is. Your ego cannot be bigger than your relationship."

Learning an important life lesson, Adi went to meet Natalie and genuinely apologized to her. He quietly listened to her as she vented out her disappointment. It didn't matter if he agreed with everything Natalie said or not. He quietly listened to her until her anger fizzled out. The fight ended.

The next day, Revathi saw the same cheerful twinkle in Adi's eyes. Even Natalie was her cheerful self on the morning show.

The Swarovski Giveaway

"Real people's fashion is more relatable and practical than the ramp."

Revathi loved daily fashion and accessories and used to follow real-world people and their fashion. She could relate more to fashion from real working people than celebrities and movie stars.

Revathi used to observe the clothing and accessories of real people on TV news, interviews, and documentaries. Natalie was one of them.

Natalie was always dressed fashionably and elegantly for her daily show. Revathi liked her dresses and the choice of colors. Revathi thought Natalie dressed very professionally and yet looked very stylish at the same time. For accessories, Natalie went with the theme of less is more. Natalie wore light jewelry and mixed and matched these with her clothing. Over a period, Revathi had realized Natalie had a good collection of earrings, pendants, and accessories. On her left wrist, she always wore a small women's watch with its face on the inner side of the wrist. Other accessories and jewelry changed, but the wristwatch was always there every day. Revathi inferred that it must be of some sentimental value for her. Over a period, Revathi had started recognizing all of Natalie's jewelry.

"Women these days are lucky there are so many options of precious and semi-precious accessories, that too from authentic brands that they can choose from."

"Yes, you are one of them."

"What?"

"Lucky. You have so many of these accessories and pieces of jewelry."

Revathi herself had a huge collection of accessories that she loved to wear for work.

"Yes. I am. But I mean, women did not have so many office wear, light jewelry, and accessory options when I was younger. Especially in diamonds."

"You are right. But you made up for the lost time in youth with the huge collection you have now."

"Yes, right," Revathi registered her disagreement with Harpreet's comment using minimum words to avoid a debate. The number of clothes, jewelry, accessories, and footwear a woman should own, how much was truly necessary, how much was just enough, and how much was an indulgence was the perennial topic of disagreement among couples.

One morning, following her routine, when Revathi switched to DE MEDIA while having her morning coffee, she observed an even brighter spark on Natalie's face and a twinkle in her eyes. Natalie appeared extremely happy as if she were blissfully lost in the magic of love. Revathi also noticed Natalie had a sparkling new bracelet on her right wrist.

"Someone seems to be doing jewelry shopping," she commented.

Harpreet ignored the comment as he thought Revathi was planning to buy another piece of jewelry herself to add to the humongous collection that she already had.

The previous day was Natalie's birthday. Natalie had spent the morning responding to the wishes from her friends and family. The first call she received in the morning was from her father. She spoke to him for almost 15 minutes before he handed the phone to her mother. That conversation did not last too long.

"Mum, please. It is my birthday today. Let us not talk about that today."

Though Natalie's father was the first one to call in the morning, he was not the first one to wish Natalie.

Adi had called her at 11.55 p.m. the previous night and insisted on meeting her at the café across the street from her apartment. It was unexpected for Natalie, but she was elated at the surprise call from Adi. She obliged and went to the café without asking any questions.

At the café, Adi was sitting in the external seating area outside with a bunch of red roses and a box that appeared to be a pastry laid on the table. The dimly lit street, fancy warm café lighting, and the cold breeze made the environment romantic. Love was in the air. Either that or the emotions of Adi and Natalie made the environment romantic. Maybe even if it were in the middle of a crowded train station, they would have felt it was romantic.

Adi gave the roses and lit a candle on the cake to celebrate her birthday.

"Happy birthday, Natalie."

"Thank you. This was so wonderful. The best surprise ever."

Adi then took out a box adorned with a satin ribbon and gifted it to Natalie.

Natalie wore the bracelet to work the next day.

The following weekend, during the routine video call, Revathi noticed something interesting that she never expected to see in Adi's house. That added some solid evidence to her circumstantial theory of Adi and Natalie being a couple.

Adi walked around his house while chatting with his mother. He walked back and forth from his living room to the bedroom and then to the balcony and back. Most of their video calls went this way.

"Mr. Comet!"

Revathi used to tease Adi because Adi could never sit still. He would wander in the house and love to go outside on long walks.

As Adi crossed his bedroom, Revathi observed a paper bag lying on Adi's desk in the corner of her phone screen. It was hidden behind some books but did not escape Revathi's sharp eyes. Revathi noticed a Swarovski Swan with Swarovski written underneath it on a trademark indigo-colored Swarovski paper bag. The image was pixelated, but she could never miss a Swarovski. Revathi was excited as if she had solved a great mystery. During Adi's next pass in the bedroom, she carefully checked and confirmed it was a Swarovski paper bag they gave in a Swarovski store to carry the jewelry bought there. It was.

While still on call with Adi, Revathi quickly browsed the Swarovski website on her laptop. A few clicks later, a white rose charm bracelet appeared on the screen, like the one she had seen on Natalie's wrist earlier that week. Revathi could not hide her excitement but did not want to reveal her discovery to Adi. She made an excuse to Adi to end the call sooner than usual so that she could share her discovery with Harpreet. Harpreet was enjoying his weekend afternoon sleep. Revathi was too excited to wait for Harpreet to wake up. To Harpreet's annoyance, Revathi woke him up from his afternoon slumber and narrated her discovery to Harpreet. Still groggy from his deep afternoon sleep, Harpreet could only partly understand what Revathi was telling. It took a while before Harpreet could understand the whole thing.

"Technically, this would also be considered as circumstantial evidence."

"Yeah, right."

"Enough of your technical assessment. I am right, and you know it."

The proof was conclusive, and Harpreet was convinced about Revathi's hypothesis that Natalie and Adi were a couple.

"Yes, you are right. Wow. I am proud of you. The way things are going, wait for a few days, and you might see an engagement ring on her finger," Harpreet mused.

Revathi hugged Harpreet in excitement. She was happy that her son had found love again.

I Want to Meet Her

Revathi was looking at the agenda and brochure of the international conference on Psychology and Allied Sciences that she received over email. The conference was focused on psychological, emotional, social, cognitive as well as behavioral sciences and their applications. She was in her office at the institute, and two of her PhD scholars sat in front of her with their requests.

"Madam, it would be great if you could join us at the conference."

Her PhD scholars were presenting papers at the conference and hoped their guide would join them. They also hoped to get an evening free away from their guide to party and do some pub hopping.

Revathi was a renowned professor of psychology and social sciences. She had attended several conferences during her career that spanned over three decades. As a renowned psychologist and author of bestselling books, she has also presented lectures and has been a keynote speaker at several of these conferences. Visiting conferences was common for Revathi, with her students presenting papers each year at several international conferences. She was a co-author on most of those papers.

Revathi would travel to some of these conferences but preferred to skip most as it would require too much and frequent travel.

Revathi was contemplating whether to attend the conference. It was a long journey to Turkey for a two-day conference.

"I am not promising anything; let me think about it," Revathi avoided the request without disappointing her students.

It had been a week since the student's request. Revathi had not given travel a second thought. It was a Sunday morning.

Harpreet was preparing his morning coffee while Revathi was seated in front of the television as Natalie narrated the morning news on a Sunday morning special television show. Sunday mornings were special and more relaxed. Sundays started with morning coffee. While her husband sat going through the newspaper, Revathi relaxed in front of the television or in the garden. Later, they had an elaborate breakfast, late, as compared to every day. Then a late lunch. Harpreet loved his afternoon sleep on Sunday, while Revathi loved spending the afternoon reading or occasionally enjoying a good movie.

The coffee was ready; Harpreet poured two cups and carried them to the living room where Revathi was sitting. As she sipped her coffee, she heard Natalie say, "I am going to do a special documentary on the psychology of modern love. As a part of that, I will be attending the International Conference on Psychology and Allied Sciences in Turkey. The report will cover views of world-renowned psychologists on the topic in addition to several other aspects. So, stay tuned for the documentary, which will be released next month."

Revathi was intently listening to what Natalie was narrating. Her mind went into overdrive as she looked at Harpreet. Harpreet looked back at her. He knew the look in her eyes and started nodding his head sideways in disapproval.

"No, don't even think about it. You are not meddling with this."

"I am just going to go and meet her. I will just try to get to know her better."

Moments ago, Revathi was convinced of not going to the conference. Now, she felt otherwise. Harpreet knew that once Revathi had made up her mind, no matter what he did, Revathi would not back off. Trying to convince her would lead to an argument that he could not win. Harpreet decided to conserve his energy instead and avoid spoiling Sunday.

Sunday was still going to get spoiled. What would have been a leisurely Sunday transformed into a travel preparation sprint.

"Still, there is time. I will call my travel agent; he will help arrange the tickets and visa."

Throughout the day, conference registration was done, tickets were booked, and visa documents were collected. Harpreet was confident she would get a visa in time for travel.

Revathi was excited and looked forward to meeting Natalie—his son's girlfriend, possibly his future wife.

That evening, when Adi called, she also talked about her plans to visit Turkey for the conference.

"You are more than halfway there. You could extend your trip and visit me in Germany, Amma."

"Maybe I will."

Adi couldn't figure out the cryptic answer that Revathi gave. He decided not to probe.

"Which conference are you attending?"

"International Conference on Psychology and Allied Sciences."

Listening to this, Adi was tempted to talk about Natalie and her plans to visit the same conference. However, Adi decided not to and fumbled for words, unsure what to say while this thought ran through his mind.

"Good... Good... I ate a sandwich for lunch. Did you have your dinner?" It was still 6 p.m. in India.

Adi had the habit of filling silence with the word "Good."

Revathi noticed Adi's struggle to hide his thoughts and failed attempt to salvage the situation with an unrelated question. Revathi smiled to herself and decided to have fun with Adi.

"It's only 6 p.m., Adi. By the way, do you know anyone who is traveling to the conference during the same period as I am? I would have carried some sweets and handed them to her to give them to you."

Revathi intentionally used "her" instead of "him". She also intentionally asked anyone traveling to the conference specifically. Adi panicked listening to the specificity of the question, as he would have to lie.

Adi hesitated and muttered quietly, "I don't know. How would I know anyone going to the psychology conference, Amma?"

"Are you sure?"

"Why would I know anyone, Ma? I will let you know if anyone is attending the conference," Adi was now irritated.

Revathi smiled to herself at Adi's dilemma and irritation.

News of Revathi's travel to the conference was spreading and causing various reactions and emotions among those who came to know about it. Shefali was happy that her guide was joining them for the conference, while Rohit and Surabhi wanted a trip without adult supervision.

Her other students were happy to get more time on their assignments as Revathi was traveling, while the conference organizers added her name to the list of renowned academicians' attendees along with several others attending the conference on their portal.

Adi had his own dilemma, whether to tell Natalie about his mother's travel to the same conference she was attending. He knew Natalie would be excited and would love to meet his mother. Adi wasn't ready for it. He decided not to tell Natalie. This was not going to stop Natalie from knowing that Dr. Revathi Iyengar was going to attend the International Conference on Psychology and Allied Sciences in Turkey. In the professional circle, Dr. Revathi Iyengar Sodhi was known by her maiden name, Dr. Revathi Iyengar. Revathi had maintained that to have her individual identity. Not to burden Adi with two last names, Harpreet and Revathi had decided Sodhi as his last name. Natalie would have never guessed Aditya Sodhi was the son of Dr. Revathi Iyengar.

Revathi was going through her own dilemma.

"I am still not sure how I will be able to meet Natalie. There are more than 1000 participants, and she probably would be busy with her media work."

"Just walk over and talk to her."

Revathi felt there was merit in Harpreet's suggestion, provided she finds Natalie at the huge conference.

"Maybe the event dinner could be a good opportunity. Not everyone enrolls for it, so the crowd is less. I hope Natalie enrolls for the dinner."

"I would still suggest not to meddle in this, let Adi's story run its own course. Do not try to influence."

"I am not influencing anything; I just want to meet her and get to know her."

Harpreet could sense anger and irritation in Revathi's tone as she said this. Harpreet decided not to push his point further.

A day later as Revathi was checking her email at her office in the morning, she noticed an email from Natalie Schmidt. She couldn't believe her eyes. Was it a coincidence? Was it a SPAM? Why would she get an email from Natalie? Several thoughts ran through her mind. Revathi hurriedly opened the email to read its content.

Dear Dr. Revathi Iyengar,

I am Natalie Schmidt. I am a reporter and a presenter at a German media and news channel, DE Media. I am doing a documentary titled Psychology of Romance. As one of the world-renowned experts in psychology and the author of the bestselling book Psychology of Courting, your input would be valuable to my documentary. I would like to make an appointment for an interview during your visit to the International Conference on Psychology and Allied Sciences in Turkey.

Hoping to hear back from you.

Yours Sincerely,
Natalie Schmidt

As part of her preparation, Natalie was going through the list of renowned attendees who were attending the conference. In the list, she found the name of Dr. Revathi Iyengar. She was excited about the possibility of interviewing her in person. Earlier, she had thought of interviewing her remotely.

Turkish Delight

"Here's your key, your room number is 301."

The receptionist at the hotel handed over the keycard to Revathi.

Her students were placed in nearby rooms. Surabhi and Shefali shared a room, while Rohit had the luxury of a separate room.

Her work had taken her all around the world; however, visiting Turkey was the first time for Revathi. They had a comfortable flight from Mumbai to Istanbul and then a connecting flight from Istanbul to Adana. Adana is a large city in Turkey near the northeastern corner of the Mediterranean Sea.

Revathi's interview with Natalie was scheduled for the next afternoon. Revathi was eager to meet Natalie and couldn't wait to see her. She wondered if Natalie had already arrived and whether she should reach out to her. Natalie had shared her cell phone number via email to be able to connect, if necessary, at the conference. Calling Natalie and appearing too eager to meet her would seem weird and peculiar to Natalie, she thought. Revathi decided to turn in and spend the rest of the evening in the room instead. Her students decided to go out and explore the city.

Natalie had arrived at the venue that afternoon and was staying at the same hotel as Revathi. It was one of the recommended hotels listed on the conference website.

Revathi reached the venue of the interview 15 minutes before the scheduled time. It was a temporary office that DE MEDIA had booked to film the interviews at the same hotel. Natalie had just concluded her previous interview with another renowned psychologist, who had left. Natalie was sitting at a desk making some notes from her previous interview as Revathi entered the office. From the waiting lounge, she saw Natalie through the glass wall.

"She looks smarter and prettier in person than on TV," Revathi thought.

Revathi stood there watching Natalie for a few moments before she knocked on the makeshift studio glass door. It was a big room with a camera set up in front of the sofa and chair. Natalie looked at the door and quickly got up to greet Revathi.

"Thank you, Dr. Revathi, for finding time for this interview."

The familiar sound that Revathi had heard hundreds of times on television greeted her in person.

"The pleasure is all mine, dear. I was excited to receive an email from you and participate in the documentary of a famous media personality."

Natalie was impressed by Revathi's humble response and felt a little more relaxed. She looked at Revathi in disbelief at her comment on a famous media personality.

"No, really. I have a confession to make. You wouldn't believe me, but I love watching foreign news channels, and trust me when I say this: I have been watching your news hour show every day for quite a while. You are remarkable and have quite an impressive show there."

Natalie almost blushed, listening to such kind words about her from a world-renowned psychologist. She wouldn't have ever imagined she was known to people in India, and even more so, Dr. Revathi watched her show every day. Such calm, friendly composure from Dr. Revathi triggered a sense of closeness and appreciation from Natalie.

"I have a confession of my own," Natalie responded.

"I am a big fan of your book *Psychology of Courting*. You have captured the never-written-about view on relationships so well. It opens a totally different perspective on love and relationships."

The power of admiration is often undervalued, and it is an art that most people lack, either out of ego or simply awkwardness to say words of praise to someone. Genuine admiration can help build trust, understanding, and mutual respect, creating a strong and healthy bond between individuals.

With this initial conversation, Natalie and Revathi got comfortable in each other's company and started chatting while the DE MEDIA technical person returned and arranged for the next interview.

The interview concluded. Natalie and Dr. Revathi continued chatting after the interview was over. Natalie's next interview was due in a few minutes, but both wanted to continue their conversation.

"What are you doing this evening? I do not want to intrude, but we could meet for dinner if you are free," Revathi asked.

Natalie was glad to hear the offer and agreed.

It was a long and busy day. As she finished her day, Natalie was eager to talk to Adi and tell him about her day and the multiple interviews she took. Unlike Adi, Natalie liked to talk to Adi about everything that happened in her life and narrate everything in detail. Adi was the quieter one. She called him as soon as she reached her room. They exchanged pleasantries and then Natalie went straight to talking about her day. She was excited to share about all the great people she interviewed that day. Specifically, she was eager to talk about Dr. Revathi.

She had not had a chance to talk about the people she would interview in Turkey before traveling.

"You won't believe whom I interviewed today. The one and only author of *Psychology of Courting, Dr. Revathi Iyengar.*"

Adi spluttered, mouth full of water, all over the room as he heard this. He was drinking the water with his phone on speaker mode as he started talking to her. He couldn't believe it.

"Why... Umm... I mean, how?" he muttered what he was thinking in panic.

He did not want his mother to meet his girlfriend. He felt that would lead Natalie to believe he wanted to marry her. Let alone making a commitment, Adi would avoid even the smallest gesture that would imply his interest toward something he was not convinced to commit. Adi's brain was wired to work against any such thing unless he was convinced of fulfilling it. Several months back, when Natalie had seen the book written by his mom at his home, he had pretended he did not know the author. It was because he knew that she would have insisted on talking to her. She was a big fan of Revathi's book.

"She is an amazing person, so down to earth, so intelligent, so good to talk to," Natalie went on for almost 10 minutes talking about her conversations with Revathi and praising her. Adi was tempted to tell her that Revathi was his mother and take pride in it. It was very tempting, but he refrained from it. He realized it was too late now. He would end up in big trouble if he told Natalie about it now. Natalie had big expectations and do's and don'ts for a boyfriend. "As a boyfriend, you should not be hiding things from me. Especially such an important thing." These were the words from Natalie when he had lied to her to get out of an art exhibition to go to a movie with his friend. These words echoed in Adi's ears. It had led to a big fight, and it took Adi several days of hardships to calm Natalie down and bring her again to speaking terms.

Adi realized that if he told his mother now, he would not hear the end of it. By not telling her that Revathi was his mother, he had dug himself into a hole with no way out. He had no excuse.

Adi was now very worried about how this was going to turn out, so he decided to keep quiet for now.

"I am so excited to meet her for dinner again. Need to get ready now. Bye. Love you."

"Bye. Love you too," he did not hear a word Natalie said on the phone as his mind worried about the grave problem.

Revathi carried herself gracefully and elegantly in the beautiful beige saree, a prominent bindi on her forehead, and a simple yet stylish diamond pendant on her neck. She had a watch on one wrist and a bracelet on the other. The confidence with which she wore her native dress in a foreign land without feeling out of place made it look even prettier. Natalie was already seated in the restaurant. She was impressed and inspired, watching Revathi walk in confidently in her saree.

Earlier in the hotel lobby, Rohit and Surabhi were ready to go out sightseeing and have dinner at the local bar in the evening. Shefali wanted to go too. However, she was worried about what Revathi Ma'am would think if they went out alone, leaving her behind.

"What are you guys doing this evening? I am going to have dinner with Natalie Schmidt."

"Surabhi and I are going for sightseeing and dinner."

"What about you, Shefali? You are not going?"

Shefali hesitated. "No, it's okay. I am staying back. We can have dinner together."

Revathi wanted to have dinner with Natalie alone; she had her own devilish plans. The last thing she wanted was her student meddling around, though Revathi did not want to shoo away Shefali directly.

"Okay, good. We can review the notes I gave you for your paper presentation tomorrow. You can expect some of those questions and better be prepared."

Shefali looked at Revathi in disbelief as Rohit and Surabhi burst into loud laughter and mocked Shefali for the fate that she had brought upon herself. Of course, the laughter and mocking were inside their minds. They couldn't wait for Revathi to go away so that they could mock Shefali in real.

"We'll have dinner at the hotel restaurant at 8 p.m.," Revathi said. She walked away to allow Shefali some time to recover from what had just happened and let Rohit and Surabhi talk some sense into her. After much mocking from Rohit and

Surabhi, Shefali still did not have the courage to change her plans and tell Revathi.

"What will Ma'am think about me?"

"Nothing," Rohit and Surabhi both replied loudly in chorus.

"Ok, fine, use our names that we are insisting on you going. Just tell her we have already prepared for those questions."

After coaxing her for 10 minutes, Shefali gathered the courage to go and tell Revathi.

"Ma'am, I think I will go with Surabhi and Rohit if it is okay with you."

"Okay," Revathi got what she wanted.

Natalie was dressed in a casual yet elegant white top, maroon skirt, and matching sandals. Revathi could identify the Swarovski bracelet that she had seen Natalie wearing earlier on the television. Revathi smiled, remembering the Swarovski bag that she had seen at Adi's place during their video call.

"Your bracelet is beautiful."

"Thank you."

"Special gift from someone?" Revathi intentionally probed to see Natalie's reaction to the question.

Natalie fidgeted with her bracelet, forming a loop around her finger, seeking comfort in the delicate metal. Avoiding eye contact, she gazed shyly downwards. Struggling to conceal her feelings, her fidgeting with the bracelet unwittingly revealed the emotions she aimed to keep hidden.

"Yes. It is a gift from my boyfriend for my birthday."

For a modern, smart, and confident girl like her, she seemed remarkably self-conscious about admitting that she had a boyfriend. It displayed the profound love and emotional investment she had for her boyfriend.

"Ah. Okay. It is beautiful," Revathi kept her response casual, not to embarrass Natalie by probing further. She decided against revealing her knowledge of her boyfriend.

They ordered food and started conversing on multiple topics. Natalie was mostly interested in Revathi's book.

"Fundamentally, men and women are wired the same globally. It does not matter which country or culture they belong to."

"But culture would matter. Isn't it? The habits, customs, religion, and way of life would differ largely."

"You are right. They differ. It is not a one-dimensional view. We need to look at all aspects and understand whether they are attributes of an individual or if they are attributes of a culture or society."

Natalie was intrigued by the comment and attentively listened to what Revathi was saying.

"I will explain, but you need to start eating. You are so engrossed in our conversation that you haven't even started." Both laughed.

"Habits and personality are attributes of an individual and would play a major role in a relationship, irrespective of the culture. These are very personal things. While customs are societal."

Natalie was absorbing everything about her and Adi's relationship in the backdrop. Revathi knew the reason for Natalie's curiosity on the topic but did not reveal it to Natalie.

"You would be surprised to know, contrary to popular belief, that individual attributes like habits and personality play a bigger role in making or breaking a relationship than societal attributes like culture, language, nationality, etc. Of course, this is true provided individuals have the maturity to identify the societal attributes and keep them out of the relationship."

"This is very interesting."

"But your curiosity on the topic tells me your boyfriend is from a different culture than you," Revathi intentionally poked Natalie.

"Yes, he is," Natalie was impressed.

"Well, I do not want to turn this into one of my class lectures."

Adi did not have the slightest idea that his mother and his girlfriend were having dinner together and had developed quite a camaraderie. He called Revathi to enquire about her trip. Revathi and Natalie were still having their dinner and chatting. Revathi had a smile on her face seeing Adi's call; she always did. This one was special due to the quirkiness of the situation.

"Do you mind if I take this call, please?"

Natalie nodded in affirmation.

Revathi received Adi's call. Adi inquired about her journey and the day in Turkey. Revathi replied concisely without all the details that she would typically talk about.

Revathi felt it was a funny situation that her son was on a call with her and his girlfriend sitting opposite her, both unaware of this. She decided to have some fun with her son. Revathi switched the call to a video call, and unsuspecting Adi accepted it. Video calls were a routine practice for them.

"I am having dinner with Natalie Schmidt. She is sitting right here with me," Revathi could see Adi's face literally turn red when he heard this.

For a moment, Adi blanked out. Then, gaining his composure, he responded.

Adi had a great presence of mind. He started speaking in Tamil when he realized Revathi was with Natalie, and she could hear him speak on a video call. Usually, they talked in English with some Tamil in between. Revathi felt proud of her son's smartness and smiled to herself. She continued speaking in English. Undeterred, Adi continued in Tamil, eager to end the call.

Natalie felt the voice was familiar for a moment, but with Tamil, she couldn't place it correctly.

"Mum, you are in the middle of something. I will call you later."

"No, that is fine. She doesn't mind. I will introduce you." To tease Adi, Revathi pretended to turn the phone as if she was giving the phone to Natalie to introduce her to Adi on a video call. Adi turned red with fear as if his worst nightmare was coming true—coming face to face with Natalie and being introduced as Revathi's son.

"Mum, you are at a restaurant in front of a renowned personality. Don't start talking on a video call; why are you on the phone? It is impolite. Let us talk later."

He disconnected the call.

"Sorry about that. It was my son."

They talked for an hour more about various topics before calling it a day.

Childhood Buddies

Adi was very nervous after the call with his mother. He wished he could do something about the situation, but he could do nothing. Adi called up his friend Sameer.

"I am in a soup. I don't know what to do," Adi sounded anxious.

Knowing Adi for several years, Sameer sensed the anxious nervousness in Adi's voice whenever he was in trouble. Adi continued ranting about Turkey, Natalie, and his mother. Sameer could not understand anything.

"Calm down, let's meet at Mizo's in 30 minutes."

Adi and Sameer were childhood buddies. They had their first encounter in the school classroom and became close friends. They finished school together and luckily got into the same engineering college, though in different streams of engineering. They traversed childhood and the rollercoaster of adolescence to young adulthood together. They were there for each other through successes and disappointments in life, and with each passing year, their friendship grew stronger.

During their college years, another member got added to the inseparable duo, Malini. Malini was Sameer's classmate. Sameer fell in love with Malini almost at first sight. For Malini, it wasn't the same. Sameer was too goofy and casual for a very particular and disciplined Malini. Malini did not like him initially. But Sameer's goofy innocence grew on her; before she realized it, she fell in love with him. As the girlfriend of his best friend, Adi's friendship with Malini grew as well. They used to hang out together all the time.

After completing engineering, Sameer took up an opportunity to pursue higher education in Germany, while Adi decided to pursue a job before going for higher studies. Due to family pressure, he married Malini immediately after completing his postgraduate studies. It was a marriage at a young age, but the couple wanted it, and their parents wanted it. So it happened.

Adi and Sameer were at Mizo's, a local bar, in 30 minutes, as agreed on the call. They ordered a beer, which was served promptly. Adi gulped half a pint in one go.

"Slow down, Stallion."

"I am in a stew," Adi exclaimed.

Adi explained what had happened on the call with his mother.

"But what was your mother doing in Turkey?"

"She went to attend the conference."

"And what was Natalie doing there?"

"She went to attend the conference too."

"And what were they doing having dinner together?" Sameer enquired with curiosity.

"Aren't you listening? That's what I am explaining."

Sameer found the situation amusing and burst into laughter. Adi's tense composure made him laugh even more.

"What are the odds, your mom and Natalie, same place, same time? Wow. But why is that a problem?"

"Are you not listening at all?" Adi snapped.

Natalie had seen Revathi's book for the first time at Adi's place. Natalie was surprised to see Adi reading books, that too, about romance. Adi had given an excuse that it was a gift from someone, and he really did not read it.

"I guess your ex-girlfriend must have given you that. You need it. You are so unromantic," Natalie teased him then.

Adi was technically correct. His mother had gifted him the book's first copy, but Adi preferred not to tell Natalie that particular detail. Adi had never read the book. Though he was proud of his mother, he did not find the subject of the book interesting.

Natalie studied psychology and political science during her graduation. She found the book interesting. It was about relationships, romance, and their psychological aspects, and she loved the subject. Also, it was a bestseller that Natalie had wanted to read for some time. Natalie borrowed the book from Adi, read it, and liked it very much. Natalie would discuss several things she read in the book and praise the author on several occasions.

Adi had not told Natalie that Dr. Revathi Iyengar was his mother. It was too late to tell her now, so Adi kept avoiding telling Natalie that Revathi, the author of the book that Natalie loved so much, was his mother.

"So, tell her now. Big deal," Sameer suggested.

"I know. Right. What's the big deal? I will tell her now." Adi paused for several seconds contemplating the implications of his previous statement.

It would be a big deal. Natalie was an idealist and lived in a fairyland as far as topics like romance and relationships are concerned. She expects her boyfriend to be ideal, dependable, caring, loving, romantic, and, most importantly, honest. Lately, she had also been talking about meeting each other's parents. He did not even tell her about Revathi then. Most recently, when Adi got to know that Natalie and Revathi were going to the same conference, he did not even tell her about Revathi. If he tells her now, he will never hear the end of it. He dreaded it.

"Oh, yes. Who are you kidding? It is going to be a big deal. You are screwed, my brother," Sameer exclaimed, listening to Adi's story.

"You are in a pickle, Mr Adi," Sameer couldn't stop laughing, knowing the situation that his best friend had landed himself in.

Angry Young Woman

"This is a basic necessity."

Revathi heard someone shout at the top of her voice. The voice sounded familiar. It was Natalie.

It was a busy morning at the hotel lobby as the conference had concluded, and several guests were checking out that morning. Revathi and her students were also traveling back to India that morning. Revathi was walking out of the elevator with her bag to check-out when she heard Natalie's voice. Curious, she quickly walked toward her. Natalie was at the reception counter. A group of people surrounded her watching what was happening, and several others were standing in the queue at the reception for check-out. Revathi noticed Surabhi and Shefali standing quietly next to Natalie.

Revathi was surprised and impressed. It seemed like a stark transformation. The Natalie that Revathi had known up until the previous evening had always been soft-spoken and mild-mannered. She had never raised her voice and came across as someone with a calm personality. However, this was different. As Revathi noticed, Natalie was standing amidst a crowd, her face flushed with anger and her words sharp and loud. It was as if a completely different side of Natalie had emerged, one that Revathi had never seen before. Revathi couldn't help but wonder what had transpired to trigger such a dramatic change in her behavior. She watched in surprise as

Natalie continued to argue passionately, seemingly unafraid of the attention she was drawing from the onlookers.

Revathi knew that something significant must have happened to push Natalie to this point. She felt a mix of concern and curiosity, unsure whether to approach her friend and offer support or give her space to deal with whatever bothered her. Revathi waited and observed what was transpiring.

"Dispensers in the washroom, prompt offering at room service, and none of it chargeable. Ensure this gets implemented right away. I am going to write to your management."

"Yes, Ma'am."

"And make sure the charges are deducted from her bill. We are at the restaurant having our breakfast," Natalie asserted, pointing at Surabhi.

"Yes, Ma'am. Please proceed. I will reverse the charges and provide you with the new bill at the restaurant," the hotel duty manager tried to resolve the conflict and calm her down.

Surabhi and Shefali had come to the restaurant early, and they wanted to have an elaborate breakfast at the hotel buffet before leaving for the airport. Since there was no rush at the reception, they checked out before going for breakfast. Natalie had checked out earlier and was at a breakfast table. She had an early flight. Natalie recognized Shefali and

Surabhi as Dr. Revathi's students and offered them breakfast at her table.

Surabhi was still flustered by the charge the hotel had added to her bill, and it showed on her face.

"What happened? You seem nervous. Is there anything I can help you with?" Natalie asked politely.

"Oh, it's nothing. They unfairly overcharged for sanitary pads."

"What do you mean?" Natalie's feminist, as well as idealist antennas, were heightened as she listened to this.

"I got my period this morning. I asked the room service for sanitary pads. They sent a pack of five and charged almost ten times what I would pay at a chemist in India." Surabhi hesitated and paused for a moment.

"I suppose it is still too expensive, even by Turkish standards," embarrassed Surabhi added, not to sound frugal and cheap.

"If it is so expensive, they should at least be allowed to buy one or two instead of a pack of five. They say they cannot open the pack. They are just trying to make money out of this," Shefali ranted, visibly annoyed.

Upon hearing Surabhi and Shefali narrate the incident, Natalie's anger flared, and her inner feminist took over.

Abandoning her half-eaten breakfast, Natalie stormed away from the table to confront the hotel manager. She asked

Surabhi and Shefali to accompany her. Not wasting food is a virtue imbibed in them since childhood. Leaving a plate full of food was against their instinct for Surabhi and Shefali. Hesitantly, they followed Natalie. They feared confrontation with the hotel staff.

Bypassing the check-out line, Natalie marched to the hotel reception in the lobby, shouting in frustration, "Who's the manager here?"

She confronted him about the excessive charges and the lack of basic facilities like a sanitary pad dispenser in the washroom, citing it as a global standard. The manager's excuses about hotel policy made her angrier. Discarding the excuses, Natalie continued to scold the hotel manager for the lack of basic hygiene service that the hotel should offer. This was an issue that many women faced but often went unspoken. She even played her media person card and threatened to do a media report on the sorry state and ignorance of the hotels and society at large on fundamental female care. In a bid to prevent further embarrassment and uphold the hotel's lobby decorum, the manager agreed to her requests and promised to make necessary changes.

Revathi was impressed. They were back at the breakfast table.

"I have to say, I was really impressed with how you handled that situation back there. It takes a lot of courage to stand up against the apathy and stereotypical mindset of the masses, that too for something considered taboo. You did a great job in making sure the hotel addresses the issue. Your voice made a difference."

"Thank you, Dr. Revathi. This needs to be done. This experience is an eye-opener of how these basic things are lacking in our society the world over. I am going to do a documentary on the topic, not just limited to hotels but the society at large."

Revathi nodded in agreement, appreciating her friend's determination and dedication to making a positive change. Revathi was surprised at how Natalie was back to her composed, calm self. Moments ago, she was boiling with anger.

As Revathi observed Natalie's assertive and passionate nature, she couldn't help but wonder whether Natalie's feisty yet sweet personality might be a bit too challenging for Adi to handle. Revathi always felt her son was a nerdy simpleton. He was a little goofy as well. She hoped Natalie's personality wasn't too strong for him.

Ultimately, whether Natalie and Adi are a good match depends on their individual personalities, values, and how well they communicate and support each other in their relationship. Sometimes, contrasting personalities click.

"I wish they would," Revathi wished.

Two-Fold Problem

"Look at her, she is so cute and beautiful," Revathi was in full awe of Natalie and wouldn't stop praising her every time she appeared on the television screen.

"You are so in love with her. It appears as if she is your girlfriend more than your son's," Harpreet teased his wife as they sat having morning coffee.

Harpreet paused for a moment and then added, "Do not meddle too much in their relationship. You know it does not end well."

Revathi started to respond but stopped to avoid an argument. Revathi believed she or Harpreet had done nothing wrong earlier and that it wasn't their fault. However, Adi felt otherwise.

Revathi and Natalie had become close buddies since their encounter in Turkey. They often exchanged emails on various topics, including psychology, love, relationships, etc. Both found each other interesting and had a personal interest in each other as well. Natalie had her own relationship challenges and looked up to Revathi as a world-renowned expert for guidance. Revathi found Natalie endearing and intelligent to converse with, in addition to her wishful thinking of Natalie as her future daughter-in-law.

Revathi usually looked at her personal email after work at home. There was an email from Natalie titled *Need advice.* Revathi was curious, so she immediately read the email, ignoring the other 20 unread emails.

It had been several months since Natalie had visited her parents. She had planned to visit them after her Turkey visit, but she couldn't make it due to her daily show. Eventually, she could find some time to visit them.

Natalie grew up in a rural German town just outside Berlin. It was a typical German village adorned with quaint half-timbered houses and red-tiled roofs nestled amidst lush green fields. Cobblestone streets wound through the town center, leading to a historic church. She loved the feeling of a close-knit community where everyone knew everyone, from shops to local bakeries and seasonal markets. At heart, Natalie was still a small-town girl in a big city. She always loved to visit the place she grew up in. However, the past several visits were not as much fun. She would be excited to visit, but her mother managed to spoil the visit for her.

As always, this visit also started well. However, eventually the topic came up. Her mother wouldn't let it go. The topic of Natalie getting settled.

In Germany, no specific cultural norm dictates the age at which girls should marry. Marriage age tends to vary widely and is influenced by individual choices, cultural backgrounds, and personal circumstances. Natalie's mother was of the same opinion until a few years back. In contemporary Germany, turning 30 without being married was not typically considered late or unusual. However, individual attitudes toward marriage can vary. As Natalie grew older, her mother's opinion changed. She wished Natalie would get settled and not spend her youth alone.

This had become the bone of contention between them in the last few years whenever Natalie visited. A new fuel was added to this fire when Natalie told her parents that she was dating an Indian boy. Attitudes toward marrying a non-German individual can vary among conservative Germans, as opinions are shaped by a combination of cultural, religious, and personal values. Natalie's mother grew up in a conservative German home with strong pride in being German and maintaining familial continuity and a pure German lineage. Also, she felt marrying outside the culture was difficult and more prone to failure.

"It will not last; they are different. Our lifestyle, culture, habits, all are different."

"Mum, I love him. That's what matters."

"And when it comes to kids, how will you raise them? They will be raised as non-Germans. What about our family continuity? What about German lineage and culture?"

"I don't care, Ma. We will raise them as both Indian and German. I don't care. I don't care," Natalie, tense, shouted at the top of her voice.

"And where is this guy of yours? You haven't introduced him to us. He has not even come and met us once. He doesn't seem to be serious," Natalie was on the back foot now. She knew Marie had a point there. Natalie was under tremendous pressure on this. She had her own doubts as well, as Adi had avoided meeting her parents for quite some time now.

"When will he come and meet us?"

Natalie was almost crying now.

The strong and confident Natalie, who Revathi met in Turkey, appeared fragile and vulnerable now. Dr. Revathi wouldn't have been surprised had she witnessed this. Love and the fear of losing a loved one can do this, and Dr. Revathi understood this very well.

"He will, Ma," she screamed and rushed out of the kitchen to her room.

Bernhard, Natalie's father, heard the screaming and helplessly moved his head from side to side in disagreement. He did not want to speak and add more fuel to the fight. He knew he and Marie would end up fighting if he took Natalie's side. Over the years, Bernhard had learned that the best way to dissolve a fight is to keep quiet. Bernhard kept quiet.

Nothing was concluded on the topic during Natalie's long weekend trip to her family. The weekend went by, and Natalie traveled back to Berlin, more stressed and disturbed. It showed up on her face. If not for anyone, at least for

Revathi to notice while she saw Natalie on the morning news. There used to be a slight smile in between the news sections earlier on Natalie's face. That was missing now.

Revathi got the reason for Natalie's grim face when she read the email from Natalie. Her problem was two-fold: her boyfriend wasn't ready to go and meet her parents, and her parents wanted her to get married soon; however, they were not fine with a non-German son-in-law. She saw no way out of these issues and thought of reaching out to the world-renowned specialist on the topic of psychology, human behavior, and relationships. Not as a professional, but as a confidant whom she has gotten close to. Revathi felt sorry for Natalie, for all the emotional stress that she was going through.

World over, no matter how modern society gets, no matter how independent, educated, and self-reliant a woman becomes, she still faces challenges. The challenges that arise from the societal stereotype that both men and women should get married by a certain age, as represented by Natalie's mother. But more so because of the inherent nature of the female gender's instinct and desire to build a family and nurture.

This desire is much stronger in women. It is non-existent or feeble in the case of men. For men, producing offspring is the strongest desire, hence their interest in sex. While for women, raising offspring is important, hence the desire to create a nurturing environment, a nest, and a family is important.

This desire puts a woman at a disadvantage, the situation that Natalie was in.

Revathi's phone rang, breaking her train of thought.

Revathi felt disturbed reading Natalie's email because part of the problem was her son and his non-committal nature. She knew very well that Adi would never commit even the smallest of things. This was not out of fear of commitment but from the fact that he took his commitments too seriously. Adi did not like to be wrong or not fulfill what he had committed, however big or small. So, he used to delay or not commit until he was sure of fulfilling his commitment.

Adi also never understood that showing interest in something isn't commitment. It's an important step toward commitment. Regular shoppers would go around many shops before deciding where to buy something from. Revathi remembered, for Adi, that was very difficult. He found it extremely difficult to walk out of the shop after looking for things and liking something. Since he expressed interest, he found it too awkward to disappoint the shopkeeper and walk away.

Adi felt that meeting the parents was a big step. It was a big step. But it did not mean it was a commitment inscribed in stone that cannot change. Both Natalie and Adi had the option of not following through with engagement and marriage if they thought things were not working out for them. Adi did not understand this. In Adi's mind, such small gestures were more like binding commitments that he would abide by till the end of time. Not following through was like breaking the promise. So, Adi, in his mind, thought he did not want to give a false message to her and her parents by meeting them when he was not yet sure.

Revathi understood the reason behind Adi avoiding it; Natalie did not. Thinking through the issue, Revathi decided to reply to Natalie.

Dear Natalie,

Sorry to read about the difficult situation that you are going through. I would advise you to look at the problem objectively. That will help you reduce your stress and help you work toward solving the problem instead of being overwhelmed by it. The way I look at it, you have three problems: 1. Your boyfriend is not taking steps to take the relationship to the next level. 2. Your boyfriend is not German, and your mother is against it. 3. Your mother wants you to get married soon.

If you solve the first two, the third one gets solved.

But before addressing the second problem, resolving the first problem is important. Unless your boyfriend is ready for it, there's no use fighting the second battle of marrying a non-German. So please put that issue aside and do not stress yourself out about it ahead of time. We can get to that when the time is right. That will clear your head so you can focus on the first problem.

> *For the first problem, the best way is to talk to your boyfriend and understand the reason for him delaying things. If there are no genuine reasons, then take it head-on and give an ultimatum to your boyfriend. That will also tell you how serious he is about you.*
>
> *Do let me know what happens. I am always here to support you.*
>
> *Love,*
> *Revathi*

Revathi knew Adi was always indecisive and hesitated to commit. But a little push helped him to commit. Hence, she advised Natalie to give him an ultimatum.

Natalie was having lunch alone at her office cafeteria when she got Revathi's response. She immediately read it, eager to know if there was anything in it that would rescue her from the stressful situation she was in. Revathi's objective presentation of her own problems cleared Natalie's mind of clutter. She felt better reading the email.

She reread it on her way home after work. Natalie kept thinking about Revathi's suggestion on the approach to solving the first issue, giving Adi an ultimatum. She was not convinced. Natalie did not want to do that out of fear of losing Adi.

"What if Adi broke up with her if she gave him an ultimatum?"

Natalie was not ready for that. She loved him too much to lose him, and she communicated that to Revathi.

Revathi knew that if Adi was given an ultimatum in the right way, with a mix of love, emotion, and assertiveness, her son would come through and act. But there was little chance; if the ultimatum was not delivered right, he might feel cornered, he might rebel, and break up with Natalie. Their relationship may never recover from that. Knowing how serious Natalie was about Adi, Revathi wanted to avoid that risk.

Dear Natalie,

I understand your fear. Do not give the ultimatum. Give it some time. It will all fall into place. Meanwhile, stop talking about the topic to your mother to avoid stress.

Do not worry. I will take care of it.

Love
Revathi

"I will take care of it," Natalie was intrigued and not sure what the line meant.

German Sojourn

Revathi was staring at an email from Shefali, which listed two conferences on her screen.

1. Humanities, Psychology, and Social Sciences, Berlin, Germany. May 18-20
2. 11th European Conference on Positive Psychology, Innsbruck, Austria, June 3–5.

Earlier that morning, Shefali and Surabhi were sitting in front of Revathi in her office. "Find me a conference in Europe, preferably Germany, in the next month."

They were confused about why they were suddenly asked to find a conference in Europe, but they were hopeful that they might be able to go as well on university expenses.

Their job description included assisting guides with undergraduate and postgraduate students' activities like laboratory work, assignments, and examinations. With PhD students, it's a long-duration association between students and their guide. PhD students, over a period, become like a guide's extended family. Revathi had even imagined both these girls as her daughters-in-law. She was not serious about it, nor would she act on her imagination to make it true. But the mind wanders, and it gives pleasure to do some wishful thinking. She enjoyed imagining it. She had even selected one over the other in her mind as her daughter-in-law. It certainly was imagination. It did not affect her impartial treatment toward both.

With close association over the past three years, Revathi did not find it out of place to ask them to find a conference, and Surabhi and Shefali did not mind Revathi's request. Shefali and Surabhi obliged.

"Yes, madam, any specific conference?"

"No, as long as it is related to psychology and is in Europe."

Shefali and Surabhi informed Rohit about Revathi's conference request. Conspiracy theorist Rohit immediately started telling stories.

"It's intriguing. Over the last three years, Ma'am didn't attend any conferences, and back-to-back two conferences this year. That too in Europe."

"Turkey is in Asia, not Europe, idiot," Surabhi retorted with a soft tap on the back of his head.

"It is."

The comfort that Surabhi and Rohit shared was more than friendship. A romance had started brewing between them after the trip to Turkey.

Revathi had a tough choice to make. Revathi continued to think about the two choices and the challenge she had in front of her as she left her office and started driving back home. Whether to attend a conference in Berlin or in Innsbruck. Her motive for going to Europe was to be in Berlin and straighten out what was going on between Adi and Natalie. She wished that she could talk some sense into Adi and Natalie's mother and everyone would live happily ever after. At least as far as Natalie and Adi's story is concerned. Revathi felt it would be convenient to go straight to Berlin, finish her work, and return. Innsbruck would be unnecessary additional days and extra travel.

However, there was a problem. She had to make Harpreet and Adi believe that the trip was genuine. Harpreet knew her too well to fall for the conference excuse, but Adi would. Even for Adi, if she attended a conference in Berlin, all of it would appear too convenient to believe.

Innsbruck sounded more convincing. It was a good story that would work with Adi. It was a nice cover-up—She wanted to attend a conference on "Positive Psychology" as it was an upcoming area in psychology and was of her interest. It really was. The conference was in Innsbruck. While she was in Europe, she would visit Adi for a few days in Berlin and do some sightseeing around Berlin.

By the time Revathi reached home, she had made up her mind.

As soon as she reached home, she announced her plans to attend the conference on Positive Psychology in Innsbruck and she would spend some time with their son in Berlin.

Harpreet was making coffee in the kitchen. He poured a cup for Revathi as well.

Harpreet figured out that it was an excuse to visit Adi and meddle with his life. Revathi knew he would. Harpreet felt it was meddling, while Revathi believed she was facilitating the two people in love by giving a small nudge in the right direction.

"There's no harm in that," Revathi would say whenever this topic came up between Harpreet and Revathi.

Harpreet tried to persuade Revathi not to visit Adi while they had coffee on their balcony, enjoying the evening breeze. Revathi was determined, so Harpreet gave up. Once the dispute was behind them, Harpreet started planning her trip and helping her with her travel arrangements.

As planned, Revathi arrived in Berlin from Innsbruck, and Adi went to the train station to receive her. They were elated to see each other. It had been three years since they had last met. It was when Adi had visited India during the year-end holiday season. They took a subway to Adi's house, which was a two-bedroom apartment on the fourth floor of a modern building.

The conference in Innsbruck was interesting, and Revathi enjoyed attending it. They had lectures from world-renowned scholars on topics that were relevant to modern society. Innsbruck to Berlin was a quick seven-hour train ride with a change in Munich. Revathi took a halt in Munich for twodays for sightseeing. She always wanted to visit the beautiful Neuschwanstein, the Disney castle.

Adi was excited like a kid for his mother's visit. He always thought of this and wanted to show her everything: his house, where he worked, beautiful Berlin, and the countryside. However, the situation was a little complicated now, making him anxious and tense.

When Revathi's plan was confirmed, Adi became very worried and anxious as his mother might come face to face with Natalie. He immediately called Sameer to Mizo's to discuss his problems with his best friend.

"What is the problem? You sounded desperate?"

After gulping down two sips of beer, Adi replied.

"Mom is coming."

"Wow, Taiji is coming, that's great. When?" Sameer paused for a moment and then continued. Due to his Punjabi roots, he used to call Adi's parents Tayaji and Taiji.

"And hold on. Why is that a problem? You should be happy. You always wanted them to visit."

"Put 2 + 2 together, Sameer. If they meet, Natalie will know that Dr. Revathi is my mother, and I did not tell her despite getting so many opportunities."

"Eventually, Natalie would know. It is better she knows when Taiji is around."

"How?"

"She is fond of Taiji. So she will be a little less mad at you, and things will get sorted out sooner. It is good that Taiji is coming."

Adi saw some sense in Sameer's argument, which almost brought a smile to his face. But then it disappeared again.

"What you are saying makes sense. But you know how it is with Mum," Sameer was staring at Adi, not getting the point.

"And there is Natalie. And you know how she is," Sameer was still blank.

"How can you be so naive, Sameer? It's like you know nothing about me."

'What?' Sameer was busy having fries as he tried to figure out what troubled Adi.

"Buddy, Natalie wants to meet my parents."

"So?"

"And Mum wants me to get married."

"Oh yes," Sameer paused, thought for a moment, and then said, "I still do not understand where the problem is."

"You don't see a problem with this?" Adi was getting very frustrated and angry at Sameer.

"Amma and Natalie would plan my wedding and send me an invitation on when and where I need to be present for it. That is if I survive Natalie after she knows about Dr. Revathi. I do not want to get married so soon."

"Oh, okay. Now I get it!" Sameer exclaimed as if there was a moment of enlightenment.

"I do not want to mess things up with Natalie, and I do not want to get married so soon as well. And I am sure if Amma is here, either of the two will happen."

Adi paused for several moments, staring at his beer glass. His eyes were almost moist. "You know what happened with Rashi."

"Buddy, it was not her fault, and you know it," Sameer said, putting the beer down on the table and looking at Adi tensely.

"Let go of that, Adi. It's not cool," Sameer's tone was serious.

There was silence for several minutes before Adi broke it.

"Still, Sameer, I am not ready, and it would be best if they did not meet. It's a matter of two weeks. Will you help me or not?"

"Of course I will. I am your friend. But you are being stupid about all this."

"Let us plan for Saturday."

"It may not be possible at the weekend, dear."

Revathi wanted to visit Natalie's family, specifically her mother, but in Natalie's absence. It would help her communicate freely with Marie and accomplish what she wanted to. With Natalie around, Marie would not let her guard down. Seeing the German countryside town was her excuse. Revathi had expressed her interest in one of the email conversations with Natalie after the Turkey visit. Natalie had offered Revathi to take her to her hometown and invited Revathi to visit Germany. The earlier conversation came in handy as an excuse to visit her town and meet Marie.

"I must work on other days. With television, unfortunately, I cannot skip work."

"Don't worry. I will go by myself. I love traveling alone. We will catch up here in Berlin on Saturday."

"Sure, Dr. Revathi. I will inform my mum. She will love to show you around the town."

That is what Revathi wanted: an opportunity to meet Marie alone.

"That would be helpful. Thank you for taking such good care of me."

Adi heard the last line as he walked into the living room and wondered who Revathi was talking to.

"It was Natalie."

Adi was having water. Upon hearing Natalie's name, he spat a mouthful of water on the floor.

"I told you before, we met in Turkey, and we've been good friends since then. We are meeting on Saturday."

Adi got nervous listening to this.

"I hope Natalie does not offer to come pick her up on Saturday, then she would know," Adi thought.

Adi's mind was filled with all possible ways how his secret would get caught.

'What if Natalie asks where Revathi was staying?' It is an obvious question that anyone would ask. Natalie might have already asked about this. Adi was scared and turned pale.

"What happened? Where are you lost?"

"Nothing."

Revathi told Adi about her plan to visit Natalie's town in the countryside. Adi was happy Natalie was not accompanying her. The less they met, the better.

Being a mother, Revathi knew what was bothering Adi and why he was so nervous. Revathi was enjoying it and having some fun with Adi.

"Why don't you join us on Saturday? I will introduce you to Natalie," Revathi said with a straight, sincere face. Within, she was bursting with laughter, seeing her son struggle to get out of the situation.

"No, I cannot make it on Saturday."

"You have a weekend off. Isn't it? Develop some contacts, dear. She is a celebrity."

"No. I have had a tough week. I will rest."

"Just for a couple of hours."

Adi struggled. It took him a few moments to come up with another excuse.

"Later, on Saturday, I am going out with Sameer to watch a movie."

"All of us can go watch a movie together," Revathi persisted.

Adi had no way out.

"Let it go, Amma," Adi said, annoyed, and left the room.

Revathi smiled at the plight of her son. She never intended to meet them both simultaneously and disclose the secret to Natalie that she was Adi's mother. She wanted the love story to evolve without her identity being disclosed. She was just there to facilitate. However, she was having fun teasing her son.

Secrets are more difficult to manage than truths, which can prevail by themselves and need no management. It was getting difficult for Revathi to keep track of all the equations in play, so she made a mental note of it.

1. Adi knows Revathi met Natalie in Turkey and that they have become good friends.
2. Adi does not know that Revathi knows about Natalie and Adi's relationship.
3. Natalie thought Revathi did not know who Natalie's boyfriend was as Natalie had never told Revathi about Adi.
4. Natalie did not know Revathi was her boyfriend's mother.

Revathi did not intend to change this status, at least not until everything was resolved and all hurdles to Adi and Natalie's marriage were cleared.

"What an interesting mess we have got here," Revathi thought to herself with a bit of concern showing up on her face. She hoped that everything falls in place and Adi does not have to feel the pain of heartbreak again.

As Adi walked to his room, his phone buzzed. It was Natalie. Adi immediately silenced the ring on the phone and walked out of the house.

"Amma, I am going for a walk," Seeing Adi suddenly rush out of the house upon getting a call, Revathi realized it was Natalie on the phone. She smiled to herself.

"I told you about Dr. Revathi visiting Berlin. I am meeting her this Saturday for lunch."

"Wow! Great! When?" Adi tried to show fake enthusiasm.

"Saturday," Natalie paused for a while and then said, "Why don't you join me? She would love to meet you, and even you would enjoy meeting her."

Adi could not believe what he was hearing. It was as if the universe was trying to reintroduce him to his mother and his girlfriend in the presence of both. He blanked out.

"Hello... Hello... Are you there?"

A few moments passed before Adi zoned back in.

"Yes, yes, some disturbance."

"No, you go ahead. I have some work."

"What work?" Adi had to think fast. Lame excuses did not fly with Natalie. She would question and cross-question to arrive at the root of the excuse.

Adi regretted not anticipating such situations and planning some stories beforehand to get out of them. He always believed in pressure situations; his mind worked best and delivered on expectations. He used to boast about it and give examples of the things that he felt were difficult during studies that he could solve during examinations.

Not this time. He underestimated the severity of the problem.

"What work?" Natalie repeated politely in her sweet voice, curious, not suspecting anything.

"I am going out with Sameer."

"Where?"

"Sameer is planning to buy an office; he wants to show that to me," Adi fished out an excuse from one of the conversations he had with Sameer several months ago on whether buying an office as an investment was a good idea. Adi delivered the excuse in a calm and composed tone, perfectly hiding the racy pace at which his mind was racing to stay on top of the matter. Adi was proud of himself. His mind did not fail him once more in a challenging situation.

"Okay," Natalie paused and then continued.

"Are we meeting today? I will stop by your apartment later; we can have dinner together. It's been a while since we met. You've been busy."

Adi evaded one risk only to land in another. He blanked out again.

"Hello... Hello... Are you there?"

A few moments passed before Adi zoned back in.

"Yes, yes, some disturbance."

"You seem to be getting a lot of disturbance these days," Natalie commented sarcastically, noticing the problem but not suspecting anything.

"I am going out for a drink with Sameer."

Natalie got a little annoyed now.

"Is Sameer your girlfriend? What's wrong with you?"

"Sorry, nothing. Let's meet tomorrow."

Natalie disconnected the call without saying anything.

She loved Adi dearly but felt Adi behaved insensitively, which disappointed her. Idealistic as she was, she had great expectations of how a boyfriend should be. That disappointment culminated in anger.

Adi knew Natalie was mad at him. He needed to figure something out and meet Natalie the next day, but he needed to ensure his mother was not in the way.

As always, when in trouble, calling Sameer was the mantra.

As Revathi was gathering her thoughts, her phone buzzed. It was Malini.

"Namaste, Taiji. What's going on there?" Malini inquired.

While Malini was talking to Revathi, Sameer's phone rang. Sameer's phone was in the bedroom where Malini was sitting. Irritated, Malini called Sameer to get his phone.

Malini glanced at Sameer's phone as she handed it to him. It was Adi calling.

"Taiji, something's cooking here as well. Adi just called Sameer." Both laughed at the sorry state in which Adi was.

Sameer took the phone and went out for a walk. He did not want to discuss anything with Malini, as she would tell Revathi everything.

"Sameer, you must invite Amma to stay at your place tomorrow."

"Of course. I would love to. But what's the issue?"

Adi narrated Natalie's annoyance for not meeting her and that she might visit him at his place before going out for dinner.

"I want you to have Amma for dinner tomorrow so that Natalie and Amma do not come face to face."

"Sure. I will talk to Malini; she will be happy to have her."

"One more thing. You are planning to invest in office space."

"I do. How? What? When?" Sameer reacted, confused, as he listened to Adi.

"And you are visiting one such office project this Saturday that you might want to buy and you want me to go along. So, find a project that you want to buy," Adi said, confused and worried.

Malini had been mad at him for the past several weeks because he was too busy in the office and unable to help her enough at home. Also, Adi has been very needy lately, and he had to spend more time with him to help him out.

Explaining to Malini about his movie night out that Adi had cooked up would be a tough sell. In addition, Adi suggested something for Saturday. Malini was not going to be happy about it.

"You are going to get me divorced. Stop being so needy, Adi. You are not my girlfriend."

Sameer taunted with a concerned expression, worried about Malini.

"I am in trouble, buddy. Natalie wants me to meet my Amma on Saturday. But I do not want to meet Amma."

Confused, Sameer reacts, "But she is staying with you. Why do you not want to meet her on Saturday?"

"Think, Sameer. Natalie is asking me to meet Amma."

Adi waited patiently until Sameer's mind caught up with the problem. Sameer was still lost.

"Natalie is asking me to meet Amma. She will know Amma is my Amma, and Amma will know she is my girlfriend." Adi tried to help Sameer understand the situation.

The complexity of the sentence further confused Sameer. He stopped Adi to think through the situation. A few moments later, Sameer understood the gravity of the situation and exclaimed.

"That's a terrible idea. Don't meet Amma."

"Thank you. Finally," Adi exhaled with a sigh of relief.

"So please, please, please. Help me out here. Saturday," Adi begged Sameer.

Sameer agreed, aware that he would get an earful from Malini on this.

While Adi and Sameer were talking, Revathi and Malini were busy chatting about how Adi and Natalie's love story would evolve and cooking up their own plan. Revathi updated Malini on her plans to meet Natalie on Saturday and her planned visit to Natalie's mother.

"Did you talk further to Adi about marriage?"

"Not yet; he gets angry if I do so. But I will."

Getting Adi ready for marriage would help Adi and Natalie's love story move forward. Natalie was ready; Adi had to get ready.

Both Malini and Revathi were convinced of this conclusion.

Malini concluded her call around the same time as Sameer walked into the bedroom after finishing his call with Adi. Malini taunted Sameer to stop spending so much time with Adi and pay attention to his wife and kids.

Deviating from the topic, Sameer suggested to Malini that they invite Revathi over for dinner tomorrow.

Such social norms were Malini's area, and she never expected Sameer to have enough relationship quotient to come up with such ideas. To Sameer's surprise, Malini agreed instantly. Typically, Malini would not agree to guests due to all the extra work in an already busy schedule.

Later, Malini invited Revathi to a nice dinner with the Ahujas, Sameer, and Malini.

Revathi had a wonderful dinner with Natalie that weekend. Natalie's dearest friend since childhood, Caroline, had accompanied Natalie.

"Sorry, I got Caroline along for dinner. She is my best friend, and she is in town only for the evening."

"Yes, we wouldn't miss a meeting whenever we get a chance," Caroline added.

"That's all right. The more the merrier."

Throughout the evening, Revathi noticed Natalie and Caroline's camaraderie, and she felt they would be there for each other through thick and thin.

Revathi befriended Caroline as well. The three ladies had a great time.

Adi and Sameer visited a new office building and inquired about an office space that Sameer never wanted to buy. They couldn't fake a visit, as Sameer's lie would get caught by Malini.

Mother-in-Laws Meet

Marie welcomed Revathi warmly into her house. Bernhard was out traveling to Hamburg for his work. Marie had the home to herself. Revathi also preferred that as she knew Marie would be more receptive to her thoughts and suggestions if she were alone. Revathi understood very well that when people are in the presence of loved ones, they are more stubborn and difficult. It could be due to several reasons, just to prove their point, to avoid embarrassment in front of their loved ones, or just because someone is there to mediate and take care if they let loose. Revathi always quoted an example of why siblings fight more in the presence of parents or why a child misbehaves when the mother is around.

Marie offered Revathi coffee, which she accepted.

"Why don't we sit in the kitchen while I make one?" Marie led Revathi to the kitchen.

"You've got a wonderful house. It's so beautiful." Marie smiled and thanked Revathi for her compliment. As always, appreciation was the way to people's hearts for Revathi.

"Why don't I give you a house tour before we have coffee?" Marie took Revathi around the house, backyard, and the farm.

"I have always been curious, how is it to stay in a small town in Europe? Well, in this case, Germany. I am fascinated by the picturesque countryside and picture-perfect surroundings."

Revathi wanted to have a casual conversation and develop a level of comfort before touching on a more serious topic.

Marie and Revathi chatted about multiple topics and got comfortable with each other. That was an art that Revathi knew very well.

"Does Natalie have any siblings?"

"No, she is the only one. And I have lots of dreams for her."

"I have one son as well, and I want the best for him, too," Revathi paused for a moment and then continued.

"Honestly, now I only think about him getting married and settling in life. This modern-day fad about living single and pursuing one's dreams is something I do not agree with."

The statement struck a chord in Marie's heart. Revathi knew it would; she made that statement intentionally. Marie expressed her desire to get Natalie married and settled too.

"I hope Natalie gets married and settles down as well."

"Kids these days keep their parents worried; timely marriage is the right thing," Revathi added fuel to the fire of worry that had gotten burning in Marie.

"So true."

"Don't mind me asking, but has she not found anyone that she would love to marry?"

By now, Revathi had formed a bond with Marie, especially on this topic. Marie did not hesitate to share.

"She has, but I am not sure if this boy is ready. Either he is too slow, or he does not intend to. And I feel this boy she is dating is no good. I tell you, boys these days are not good."

Revathi felt offended hearing such comments about her son and felt an urge to defend her son. She refrained from doing so.

"You know, it is easier and better if kids allow us to set them up with a match, someone whom we know, whose families we know. That way, things turn out much better."

Revathi let her guard down, listening to ill opinions about her son and took the conversation in a direction that would play against Adi's chances. She soon regretted it.

"Yes. I have a wonderful boy in my mind. Natalie dated him when they were in high school. He used to visit us often. I hear he is now a doctor and earns well. Rich family."

Revathi cursed herself for taking the conversation in the wrong direction and she needed to recover from this. She had to do that subtly and could not be too obvious by countering her own opinion moments ago.

"That would be ideal. Having her married in town and keeping her in front of your eyes in the same town always," Revathi knew that would never happen. Natalie was a career-oriented girl and would never settle in the town.

"No. The boy is practicing in Berlin. Natalie would never settle here anyway. She has a wonderful career going on in Berlin." Revathi saw an opening to come back.

"That's true. She is a world-renowned TV personality now. She shouldn't have to give up her career for marriage."

"That's true. But there is no point in all this as she loves someone else."

"Well, then pushing her into this will only make her sad. And she will resent you for the rest of your life."

"True," Marie responded thoughtfully. Marie knew it, but listening to it from someone else had a decisive impact. Hearing it from Revathi made Marie accept mentally that pushing Natalie into marriage with the doctor she was dreaming of was not a good idea and that she should not pursue it.

Revathi saw the disappointment and regret in Marie's eyes for having to let go of the idea of her coveted match for Natalie. Revathi knew she was on track again.

Revathi was done with coffee. Marie proposed to step out and go around the town and rural sites. She believed that was the intent of Revathi's visit. Revathi had gained good momentum on the topic, which was her main intention of visiting Marie. A sudden interruption from Marie broke that momentum.

Marie took her VW Beetle out and drove Revathi to the local market. It was the weekly market day. Revathi tasted and sampled some jams, spreads, and pickles made from fresh fruits. She bought some for Adi.

Later, they visited the town hall and church and took a stroll across the old medieval river bridge. Marie proudly and with childlike enthusiasm described various sites and places in her town.

Marie and Revathi talked about various topics, including life in India and life in Germany. Revathi projected a very positive picture of life in India and Indians. Indians have strong family values, and they are very accepting of other cultures as key selling points. Revathi's intent was to plant the seeds of positivity toward Indians in the mind of Marie. She knew subconsciously that the concept would grow in Marie's mind, and she would become more accepting of Indians.

It was a psychological concept. Any idea, however outrageous, if planted correctly by an unrelated source in someone's mind and given time to grow, would get far more acceptance than pushing it on someone. Corporates and governments do that by leaking some news partially before the announcements. The thoughts that Revathi shared with Marie about Indians and Indian culture were not just to impress Marie for the sake of Adi, but she believed in them.

Marie resonated with the idea of strong family values and family connections. Being an old-fashioned German, she believed in those ideas as well. She was not sure about the idea of accepting other cultures. She felt Germany had evolved since World War II and was much more accepting of other cultures now. However, she herself wasn't that accepting, especially when it came to having a son-in-law who was not German. Revathi knew the seed was planted, and it would work.

Revathi again wanted to bring the conversation back to the key topic, which Marie had earlier interrupted after coffee.

"Don't mind me asking, is this boy Natalie is dating any good? I mean, will you be happy if they decide to get married?"

"No, not at all. Yes. Maybe," Marie was caught by surprise by the sudden question. After the initial fumble, she continued.

"I mean, he is a good boy. But I feel presently it's young love. Everything is good. Later, a lot of issues will crop up." Marie paused.

Revathi waited for Marie to say more.

Marie hesitated and then continued.

"Also, he is not German. You might find me old-fashioned, but I would prefer her husband to be German. We are losing our culture and heritage. We need to preserve that."

"Oh, okay. He is not German," Revathi pretended as if she did not know about it.

"Don't mind. Nothing against Indians. But he is Indian."

"No, not at all. I understand your concern," Revathi trod carefully.

"Marrying in a different culture is challenging."

"Yes, language, food habits, lifestyle."

Revathi did not want to counter Marie directly; otherwise, Marie wouldn't be open to listening. Revathi also did not want to appear as if she wanted to convince her otherwise, so she continued with a neutral stance as if it were a normal conversation.

"You said Natalie loves him. That makes things difficult."

"It always does," Marie said in a soft, low voice, almost like a whisper. The statement seemed to carry a lot of baggage from her past.

Revathi was curious to know what that was about but refrained from probing.

Both stayed silent for a few moments, embroiled in thoughts, as they stood on the pavement in the middle of the bridge, staring at the river flowing underneath.

"You ruined everything. I will never forgive you for this." These words suddenly echoed through Revathi's mind. She felt a deep hurt in her heart that almost appeared on her face.

The baggage from the past made those few moments feel like hours for both.

"Natalie would not like it and resent you for the rest of your life if you did not accept her love," Revathi snapped out of her thoughtful silence.

"Yes. That's the reason I am unable to force anything on her."

"If the boy is decent, has no vices, and earns his own bread, then accept her wishes and support her. Marriages fail even if one marries in the same culture too, so love prevails or love fails. One cannot predict much on that."

Revathi paused and then said, "It's not worth alienating your only child over this."

"Yes," Marie nodded, seemingly convinced.

"I tell you, kids these days never fail to disappoint their parents and do exactly the opposite of what they want."

"So true," both mothers unanimously agreed on that. Revathi, too, was convinced of the correctness of that statement. Both had a hearty laugh at that. That triggered a mum conversation. It is a conversation that mothers from around the world, no matter which culture or country they are from, can relate to. Both started narrating stories about how each of their kids has habits that their mothers do not approve of. The conversation became lighter and merrier.

As they drove back, Marie said.

"Oh, I hoped so much that she fell in love with a German. But I do agree, its not worth distancing your kids from you by pushing for it."

"You can always ask them to have a second child and raise the second child in German tradition and culture."

"Not a bad idea. I might just ask that." Both had a hearty laugh at that.

***"You ruined everything. I will never forgive you for this." Revathi was jolted awake as those words played in her subconscious. Revathi took a few moments to get her bearings right.

It was a long day. Revathi was tired and dozed off on the train back to Berlin. After their excursion around the town, Marie and Revathi had a nice lunch at a local restaurant and then drove back to Marie's house. Marie dropped Revathi at the train station after coffee, just in time for her train.

In the morning, Marie was apprehensive about a stranger visiting her, and she had gotten into an argument with Natalie when she informed Marie about it. Revathi and Marie connected well after spending the entire day getting to know each other and having conversations. Being mothers, they found themselves members of a unique club where they shared similar challenges, emotions, and feelings. Through facing these common experiences, they developed a genuine and special bond.

On the train, Revathi was truly disturbed by the thoughts that played in her mind, jolting her out of her nap. All the memories rushed in, compelling her to replay them and attempt to justify what had happened again. The professional psychologist in Revathi knew that she was ruminating. But even professionals like Revathi sometimes struggle when there's an emotional connection, especially when it involves people close to her heart.

Despite a successful visit, it wasn't a pleasant train journey back for Revathi.

Successful Trip, Sad Ending

Days went by quickly, and it was time for Revathi to travel back to India. During her stay, she met Natalie a few more times. Both had grown fond of each other, and their bond strengthened.

Adi liked that his mother and girlfriend were bonding. Though he was unsure if his mother would approve of Natalie as a daughter-in-law. He hoped so as Revathi was open-minded and wasn't restrictive about social and cultural differences. While Revathi was in Berlin, she showered Adi with a lot of motherly love in the form of cooking delicious dishes that he liked. Adi would miss this when Revathi left. Despite this, Adi was relieved that his mother was leaving tomorrow, and his secret was not revealed while Revathi was in Berlin. Natalie was getting impatient as he avoided meeting her due to Revathi's presence for the past two weeks.

On the other hand, Malini was feeling a little sad as Revathi was going. Malini had gotten used to having a buddy in Berlin. Her connection with Revathi had been several years old, and they stayed connected over the phone and chat. But Malini felt having her locally was even better.

Malini had been asking Revathi to convince Adi about marriage generally, not specifically to Natalie, as it was a secret that Revathi knew about her. Malini felt at least Revathi should convince Adi to start thinking about marriage. That would trigger a stream of thoughts for Adi, and he might just start thinking about marrying Natalie. Revathi had been avoiding it.

"Taiji, you only have today. Talk to Adi."

"Yes, I will."

Revathi was scared of initiating the topic with Adi. Although she could talk comfortably with Adi about everything, she knew if she talked to Adi about marriage, Adi would get angry and stop talking to her. Adi could get very mad, and it could get ugly. This scared her.

But she had to try.

Since it was Revathi's last day in Berlin, Adi took her out for dinner. Revathi thought it was a nice opportunity to talk to Adi. While both were seated at the table in the restaurant, Revathi started the conversation.

"Adi, what do you think of getting married? Is there anyone special?"

"Amma, stop. I don't want to talk about this."

"Adi, it's been so long. You can't blame us for what happened."

Adi went silent as old memories flooded his mind. He did not want to discuss his relationship with Revathi.

"Let go of it, Adi."

"Amma, please."

Both had their dinner in complete silence, with an occasional comment on a random topic to fill the silence.

It was a sad end to a wonderful German sojourn.

Mumbai in the Past

"I need to go to the new employee induction program."

"Room 306. Take the elevator to your left."

Adi's heart raced with excitement as he entered the bustling office building on his first day of work. Nervously navigating his way through the sea of cubicles, Adi found room 306. It was already filled with around two dozen new employees ready to embark on this new adventure. Adi seated himself at one of the empty desks. It was a lengthy four-day induction program covering all aspects of the company, including company history, policies, and processes. The energy and interest in the day's proceedings gradually started dipping with never-ending lectures after the first day's excitement. It hit rock bottom by the end of the second day. By the time the fourth day approached, Adi had given up all hope and surrendered to his fate. The only ray of hope was that after the induction program ended by 2 p.m., he was supposed to meet his team. A buddy was assigned to him, who would accompany him to his new team.

As Adi got out of room 306, amidst the unfamiliar faces, one person stood out—Rashi. Rashi was fair, of average height, and slightly plump. She was soft-spoken and had a childlike innocence in her appearance that unveiled goodness of heart.

Her warm smile instantly put Adi at ease. They exchanged friendly greetings. Rashi was from the same team as Adi, a year senior to Adi. She was assigned as a buddy to help him out in case of any challenges, as Adi was a newcomer. Rashi introduced Adi to their supervisor and the rest of the team. It was a team with a lot of young boys and girls fresh out of college like Adi and some had an experience of 1-2 years in the job.

As Adi got used to the work and the work culture over several weeks, Rashi became Adi's go-to person for questions and guidance. It was laying the foundation stone for a strong friendship that was about to develop between them. Adi also made several other friends within the team. With newly gained financial freedom through the job and no responsibilities, the group of youngsters were enjoying life to the fullest. Adi and Rashi were part of the group. Weekend parties, long bike rides, trekking, outings, and movies kept the group busy. It was a never-ending celebration with the motto—work hard and party even harder. The gang was enjoying the best days of their lives. It became their go-to phrase while meeting and greeting.

"Best days of our lives, Bro."

"Yeah, BDOL, Bro."

As time passed, they all became very close friends and developed a special bond. Adi and Rashi's friendship also grew strong.

It was a restless young lot, not satisfied with the 9-5 job. Most of them were pursuing admission for higher education. The first job was a stepping stone to gain some industry experience, but it was not the destination for most of the young individuals in Adi's group. Adi was also interested in going abroad and pursuing an MBA. Adi was very clear about his goal, and he was studying for it. He had enrolled in preparatory classes to help him excel in the competitive exams and interviews. Adi hoped to secure a scholarship for his higher studies to avoid burdening his parents with the expense of studying abroad.

Rashi did not have such aspirations. She wasn't very career-oriented or ambitious. However, she loved her work and the freedom she got from earning her own money. Thinking about everyone moving on with their lives made her sad.

"The best days of our lives will not last forever."

Parent Problem

Rashi had applied for leave from the office as she was going to visit her parents for a week. Curious, Adi asked her about her visit.

"Why a sudden visit? All okay?"

Adi and Rashi were going to a movie on their bike along with the group.

"I have something to attend to. I will tell you later," Rashi deflected the question, feeling it was not the place or the time to talk about it. Adi realized something was bothering Rashi. After the movie, Adi drove Rashi back to her apartment. He stopped a little distance before the apartment to enquire about what the matter was.

"My parents have been looking for a boy for me to get married to, and I need to visit them and meet someone."

"Oh, wow!" Adi did not know how to react.

"Yes, wow!" Rashi gave a dull, lackluster, pretend exclamation.

"What is the matter? Are you not wanting to get married?"

"I don't know what I want."

"What do you mean?"

Rashi felt an urge to open up to Adi, who was her good friend, her best friend.

Coming from a traditional Marwadi family, she had not seen women in her family pursue a career. Rather, she was the first woman in her family to pursue any kind of job. She was happy about it. She loved being financially independent and the freedom that came along with it and staying away from home, just like all her young friends and peers. More recently, her traditional household had ventured into a new project of getting her married. Brought up in a traditional Marwadi family, she had seen girls married off as soon as they turned 18. With changing times, the community did progress. They waited until graduation before getting their girls married. That is at the age of 21. She was already 24. Her parents were considered too modern within the community for this. However, 25 was like a sunset age. Even her parents weren't modern enough to hold off her marriage beyond 25.

Rashi was not sure how she felt about marriage. She had grown up obeying her parents. Her parents had agreed to let her study engineering despite it being considered a male profession by their community. They also allowed her to go and work in Pune, away from home when she secured a job straight out of campus. She knew several people in the community frowned upon this. Her parents put her happiness ahead of such pressure from relatives. She was grateful to her parents for their support. She owed all that she could achieve in life to her parents. Now that her parents are asking her to get married, she feels obliged to listen to them.

"You are so intelligent and good at your work. How can they think of giving up all this?"

"They are not asking me to give up my career. They are only asking me to get married."

"It's the same," Adi reacted in frustration.

Rashi did not like the tone of Adi.

"Listen, they are not the villains here. They have supported me against all odds until this point. I have achieved whatever I have because of them. Else, I would have been married to someone when I turned 18."

Adi realized his mistake.

"Sorry, I did not mean that."

"I do not want to let them down now. They have done a lot for me."

"But giving up all this is not good."

"Well, it depends on who I get married to. I might just get lucky, and I get to continue my career," Rashi paused for some time and then added, "Oh my God, you think I must go and marry that one boy that my parents chose for me?" Rashi rolled her eyes at the pathetic thought and continued, "You do know, right, I have a say in who I marry."

"Yes. Like MCQ. You are given four choices from your community, and you must pick one. What if you want a fifth option—none of the above?" It was a serious thought, but Adi delivered it as a joke.

Rashi understood what Adi was implying, but she played along and took it as a joke.

"I guess your MBA preparation is going too well, with MCQs and all."

Both laughed superficially, not letting the deep undercurrents of Adi's comment surface.

Rashi was more accepting of the situation, but Adi was not, as he would realize in the subsequent week when Rashi traveled to Jodhpur for a week to meet the match her parents had found for her.

Since the day he had the conversation about Rashi's marriage, he was disturbed. Revathi had noticed the change in Adi's behavior. She had decided to be observant but not intervene. Adi was worried about Rashi. He did not realize why he was so disturbed and sad. He was concerned about her as she was going to give away a promising career. He felt he was disturbed since his good friend was going to move away. But it was more than that. He kept thinking about her all day.

Four days into the week, Rashi called. Adi was elated to see Rashi's name flashing on his phone screen. He enquired about the boys she had met, eagerly curious about what had happened. Though Adi did not show his eagerness to Rashi, she gave a low-energy response.

"Everyone in my family is discussing it."

Adi burst into anger listening to Rashi's response.

"Everyone in the family? Are you crazy? What are you doing, Rashi?"

Rashi was shocked by Adi's sudden outburst. She maintained her composure and deflected the topic. "Leave all that. Tell me what's happening there."

Adi talked for some time, but his mind was preoccupied.

By the next morning, Adi had decided to propose to Rashi and express his love for her.

Rashi returned on Sunday evening. Adi had already informed her that he would meet her the same evening. Rashi was happy that Adi was coming to meet her, though she was worried that Adi would probe into her marriage topic.

Adi parked his motorcycle below her apartment, and both went for a stroll in the neighborhood. After some small talk, Adi asked Rashi about her marriage. To Adi's delight, Rashi's visit was unsuccessful. She met three boys in the presence of their families in a typical arranged marriage meeting setup. She was rejected by two, and her family did not find the third family affluent enough for a match. As they walked side by side slowly, Adi asked, "So, what now?"

"Nothing, life goes on until the next showing."

Adi took this opportunity to express his wish to marry her, which surprised Rashi. She had never thought of Adi as someone she would love or marry. She was an independent girl, and marrying as per her parents' wishes was her choice.

"Adi," Rashi calmly replied as they continued to stroll through the dimly lit street.

"It's nice of you to care about me and think about me. But I do not want you to pity me and offer me marriage to save me or anything. What I am doing in my life is my choice. For my parents."

Adi was not expecting this. He had imagined a surprised but excited "YES" from Rashi for his proposal.

"It's not that. This last week I thought about it. And I really like you. I cannot lose you. I think I can spend the rest of my life with you."

Adi made several mistakes in his previous sentence. He used "like" instead of "love". Also, he said "I can" instead of "I want to". The mistakes were unintentional and reflected his lack of skills in expressing his thoughts in words eloquently. His nervousness to talk about the topic to Rashi added to the fumble. Rashi did not pick up on all such mistakes, but what she was hearing from Adi did not sound right to her heart.

They parted that evening with a promise that both would think about the idea.

Sometimes possibilities can kindle love. Rashi, who had never seen Adi as her romantic interest, suddenly had a blank canvas of possibilities in front of her. These possibilities triggered emotions that did not exist before. Adding fuel to the possibilities, Rashi imagined what it would be like to marry Adi. Adi had been a good friend, and the thought of marrying him felt exciting and fun. Despite attempts to stop it, her mind drifted into thoughts of her future life with Adi. However, Rashi was a cautious girl; putting her imagination into action was a different matter altogether. There were challenges between them and at home. Marrying someone outside the caste was unimaginable for her parents. She did not want to disappoint her parents. But that came later; the first blocker was she was not sure if Adi had proposed to her for the right reasons. Hence, she was hesitant to accept Adi's proposal.

Adi was persistent. Over the past week, while Rashi was away, Adi's feelings for Rashi gained clarity. After his proposal to Rashi, his resolve about marrying Rashi grew even stronger. After the proposal, things got a bit awkward in the office when they met. They both wanted to talk to each other and say so many things but could not in the office environment.

"I will visit your place after the office in the evening; we will talk then." Over the next few days, Adi visited Rashi daily after the office. Typically, they would take a stroll, chatting and discussing the topic. Adi tried to convince Rashi about his self-realization of his love for her. At times, they would delve into a role play as husband and wife and imagine how life would be as a married couple. And then both would laugh about it.

The conversations opened Rashi's mind to the world of possibilities of life after marrying Adi. These possibilities were gradually starting to kindle love for Adi. However, Rashi was cautious and not willing to let her guard down. She shared her concern about her family as she was so sure that her family would not accept Adi as he was from a different caste.

"Don't worry, we will find a way out."

Every evening Adi hoped Rashi would accept his proposal but had to go back disappointed. Adi persisted and would visit Rashi to convince her every evening, riding through the dense city traffic 15 km away. After several days of heartfelt conversations, Rashi was convinced of Adi's love for her, and she, too, was feeling love for Adi. However, she was confused and scared of this new emotion, and she did not want to disappoint her parents. They stopped her from expressing her love for him.

One such evening, Adi's patience gave in.

"If you don't want to marry me, I will not bother you any longer. Sorry to have bothered you for so long. Take care. Bye."

Adi got angry, got on his motorcycle, and drove away. Rashi was shocked, scared, and confused. She tried to stop Adi, but he did not stop. She started crying as she saw Adi ride away.

We only realize the value of something when faced with the risk of losing it.

Wedding Bells

"We hear Adi has got admission to an MBA."

"Yes, he really worked hard for it."

"Congratulations. When is he traveling?"

"He is going in July."

"That's two months from now. We need to hurry and finalize their wedding date. They should get married before Adi travels to the US, and they should travel together to the US."

Life was going great for Adi. Rashi was able to convince her parents about Adi. His MBA dreams as well were coming true. He had secured admission to a renowned MBA school. He was a bit sad that he would have to travel and go away from Rashi. He did not expect this turn in the story. Adi was not ready for this. He had his plan chalked out: do an MBA, secure a high-paying job, secure his career, and then get married. The request from Rashi's parents was not in Adi's plan.

Rashi's parents had agreed to their marriage for her happiness, though they did not approve of Adi. Mathura Das was very vocal about his feelings when he first met Adi's parents.

"With God's grace, we have a booming business, a big haveli in Jodhpur, and properties across several cities. All this is for

Rashi. We were looking for a wealthy family for Rashi in our community to get married."

"I can understand your emotion as a father," Revathi tried to keep things cordial, not getting offended by a comment from Rashi's father. Harpreet was offended, and he did not like it. He was angry at Matura Das's comment.

"We are not rich, but we are well-off, enough to live a prosperous and contented life."

"Our daughter's happiness is paramount to us, and hence we agreed to this match."

"For us too. We are here for Adi's happiness. Else we wouldn't be sitting here to be insulted like this."

The seeds of a tense relationship between two families were planted in their first meeting itself. It was only the parents' meeting; Adi and Rashi were not present.

Adi had overheard Harpreet and Revathi discussing their visit to Rashi's parents. He did not like what he heard and expressed his anger to Rashi about the whole event.

"Try to think about it from my father's perspective and don't feel too bad about it. He is also having a tough time accepting all this. Still, he is trying."

"Mom also tells me the same thing. Are you two ganging up on me even before we are married?"

"You never know." Both laughed.

Adi decided to let go after listening to Revathi and Rashi's advice.

Days passed, and the conflict over their getting married before Adi traveled ceased to subside. The topic was discussed among all combinations of people. Rashi talked to Adi's parents, Rashi's parents talked to Adi, and both parents talked to each other. However, there was no confusion. Mathura Das was adamant on his ask, and so was Adi. Revathi and Rashi were the mature ones who were trying to reach some settlement.

"You need to remember sacrifice was the first mantra of love and marriage," Revathi concluded her conversation with Adi, trying to convince Adi to give in. Adi and Rashi's meetings were also all about this controversy over the last several days.

"You love me, and you proposed to me. You convinced me about your love for me. Love is about sacrifice, Adi. We are in this together, and if we want to be successful at this, we need to make sacrifices for both of us."

"I am the one who must sacrifice. Where is the sacrifice for you?" Adi was agitated. Rashi responded calmly.

"It's not a balance sheet of sacrifices, Adi. At this point, our love is asking for more sacrifices from you. Maybe some other time I might have to sacrifice. Rather, I am already. Do you think it was easy to disappoint my parents and convince them to agree to marry you? It is up to you whether you believe in our love and love me enough."

Adi was impressed by how Rashi could stay calm and communicate her thoughts so assertively. The maturity in her thoughts was almost a reflection of Revathi. Though not too happy about it, Adi agreed to get married before he traveled for an MBA.

Discussions started on finalizing the wedding date. There were 1.5 more months before Adi traveled for the MBA. A date three weeks before he traveled was picked by the parents. His world had suddenly turned upside down with all the wedding talks. He could not imagine getting married so soon. But he had agreed to it and he still played along and did as he was told, participating in the wedding preparations, shopping, and other things. He was convinced that he was doing it for his love for Rashi. It was the right thing to do.

While the preparations were going on, the controversy had still not completely subsided. Rashi's father wanted Rashi to stay with Adi after they were married. Adi wasn't ready for that. He wanted to experience life as a student while he did his MBA. Also, there were financial challenges. Living as a couple would be too much of a financial burden. Rashi was trying to convince her father.

"I know you need a visa to go abroad. I am not illiterate. You can accompany him on a tourist visa initially. I have enquired.

Then we can figure something out. Until we figure something permanent, you can travel multiple times on a tourist visa."

Her father could not fathom why Adi would not want to take her along. Adi was not ready to give in on this one. It ended up in a stalemate. Both parties involved were adamant.

The stalemate was wearing everyone out, with similar discussions repeating among the involved parties. A rift had formed between the two families even before the bond was formalized into marriage.

There was tension between the families from the beginning. Adi's caste and financial status were unacceptable to Rashi's parents. Mathura Das's taunt: "This is Rashi's wish; else we wouldn't marry Rashi in a poor house," during the first meeting spoiled it for Revathi and especially Harpreet.

It even started impacting Rashi and Adi's relationship. The bliss of love was slowly wearing out under the burden of this family feud.

Rashi wished her marriage to be a happy milestone in her life—happy for her and happy for her parents as well. However, it was turning out to be exactly the opposite. She felt marriages are between families. If families don't gel together, then love will not prosper.

After thinking it through for several days, Rashi had made up her mind. They were the most difficult few days of her life.

"I do not wish to spend my life arguing with you."

"Why do you say that? We love each other."

Adi and Rashi took the usual evening stroll on the dimly lit streets near Rashi's house. There were dark clouds and thunder in the sky as if it was going to rain.

"I know we do. But is that enough?" Rashi paused. Adi waited for Rashi to finish her thought.

"Our parents do not like each other. How they feel and interact rubs off on us. You've already started resenting my father for what happened between the parents. Probably I do too."

They continued walking side by side slowly, almost as if they were dragging their feet. Rashi was using a lot of hand gestures as she usually did when she was talking, too charged up emotionally.

"Our relationship has already caused so many heartaches, and that will continue as our families don't get along. I want a life where I do not want to distance myself from old bonds to form a new one. Neither would you," Adi agreed to everything that Rashi said and was impressed again at her maturity and clarity of thought. But he did not like where the conversation was going.

"What are you suggesting, Rashi?"

Rashi stopped walking and turned toward Adi. Gesturing 'Us' with her hands, she said,

"I feel 'Us' will not work. It is best for us and our families that we part ways" she said with tears in her eyes.

The rain began pouring heavily, accompanied by loud thunder. They stood motionless, staring at each other, caught in the moment.

"What if I don't want to part ways." Adi's voice choked up as he finished the sentence. He struggled to keep his tears at bay.

"Don't do this, Adi. This is for everyone's good." Rashi tried to explain Adi, but in vain.

He hugged Rashi and kept repeating, "What if I don't want to part ways?" He had tears in his eyes. Rashi also started crying.

Several moments passed as they stood there hugging and crying, drenched in heavy rain. Rashi wanted to be in Adi's arms but she knew they would not be happy. Rashi stepped back, turned around and walked away.

"This is for everyone's good." Adi heard her say as she walked away, heartbroken.

Time passed quickly, and it was time for Adi to travel to Germany.

Over the past few weeks after the fateful last meeting with Rashi, Adi had started being quiet and reserved. He hardly talked to his parents. He made himself busy in preparation for travel to distract himself from the heartbreak. Revathi and Harpreet's attempts to cheer him up did not help.

On the day of Adi's travel, as Revathi was trying to have a conversation with Adi, he lost it.

"Both of you messed it up for me. You spoiled it for me and Rashi."

Harpreet was not going to sit back and take the blame for something they did not do. There was a heated argument between father and son. Revathi could do nothing to stop the unfortunate argument. She knew it was driven by emotions and pain, and Adi was venting out by blaming his parents. She knew Adi did not truly believe it. However, for Harpreet, it was hurtful and unacceptable to take the blame for it.

It all went silent after the argument.

They all hoped the argument did not happen, especially when Adi was leaving in a few hours. But the damage was done.

When it was time for Adi to leave, he touched Revathi's and Harpreet's feet to seek their blessings and left. Not a word was spoken.

It was a painful departure.

The Proposal

Sameer and Adi were at Mizo's having beer.

It was a weekday, and Adi was surprised when Sameer called Adi earlier to meet at Mizo's.

"It's Wednesday. Is everything alright?"

"Yes. Just want to take a break. It's all going very hectic."

Two hours later, they were at Mizo's.

"How did Malini allow you to do this on a weekday?"

Malini and Sameer got married four years ago. They were college sweethearts and in the same class. By the time they finished college, their parents knew about their relationship. They were forced to marry. At 24, they were married, and by 28, they had two kids. Sameer himself was like a kid when they got married. Malini feels he still is. Malini herself was a happy-go-lucky, fun-loving girl when she got married, just like a teenager.

Sameer got an opportunity to move to Germany through his job. He seized it, and they moved to Germany. It was a tough job to manage his career, family, and kids through his formative years after college. Malini supported Sameer through the rollercoaster life that they had over the past six years. Malini felt Sameer did a great job managing everything, but as a wife, she would never admit that in front of Sameer. They were more like friends living together than a married couple. However, after the kids, Malini had to switch to running a tight ship if all was to work smoothly.

"Yes, I have permission to have a drink for two hours. After that, I must go home and help Vivaan with his art assignment," Sameer said, making a face of dislike at that last part of the sentence.

"Who told you to have two kids in three years?" Adi teased Sameer.

"They are God's gift. We accepted the gift with open arms."

"God's gift or laziness to put on a condom."

Their friendship went back a long time. Adi teased Sameer. Such teasing was common between them, and they never got offended.

"No, but seriously. Malini and the kids are the best thing that could have happened to me. It gets better."

Sameer started to say, "It gets hectic and difficult at times," but paused. He had called Adi to meet for a purpose; he did not want to say anything negative about marriage.

"I am happy for you and Malini. What you have is wonderful."

Sameer felt it was the perfect cue to start the topic of Adi and Natalie's marriage without him suspecting anything.

That was the main purpose of meeting Adi today. Malini had allowed Sameer to go for a beer outing on a weekday only for this reason, and Malini was rather excited about it.

Malini had little trust in Sameer to do this right. There were days of preaching and practicing how the conversation with Adi should happen.

"Tell me, how are things between you and Natalie? What's next?"

"She is a great girl. I love her dearly. All is perfect," Adi paused for a few seconds.

"But lately, Natalie seems a little lost. I am not sure why. But she isn't herself."

"Why do you say that?"

"Well, we meet, go out, talk. But not like before. She feels lost. I cannot say what exactly is bothering her."

"Did anything happen? Did you two have a fight?"

"Nothing worth mentioning. Small stuff. Has she lost interest in me? Is she going to break up with me?"

Adi made it easy for Sameer to bring up the marriage topic. Sameer was worried about how he would bring up the topic abruptly; Adi would suspect a setup to woo him into marriage. He did not want Adi to go into a shell of negativity, which he did when Adi felt he was being pushed into something.

"Natalie wants to take this further. She is serious about you. But you are not taking any steps to make her feel that you want the same."

Adi was surprised at how confidently Sameer pinpointed the issue as if Natalie had told him about it.

"How do you know?"

Sameer realized that he had gone too directly in what he was instructed to communicate. Sameer fumbled but recovered quickly.

"Ah, I mean probably. I do not know. But I think so. What else could it be?"

Adi stared at the golden glow of the beer as light passed through it and thought for a while. Sameer took a deep breath and paused after his recovery. A while later, Adi broke his silence.

"You are right, buddy. Natalie had mentioned a couple of times that she wanted to introduce me to her parents. But I had avoided the topic."

"See, I told you. You have an easy fix to the problem. Go and meet her parents. She will be fine."

"It's not that simple. That would be sending a message that I want to marry her."

"What's wrong with that? You are serious about her. Right? She is a good girl. If you are not serious, just break it off now." Sameer stared straight into Adi's eyes as he said that. Adi was surprised at Sameer's change in demeanor. He meant what he said.

"It's not that. I am serious about her. I love her. But what if things do not work out? I do not want to give false hopes to her or her parents."

"If you are so scared, then let go of her. You do not deserve her. If you don't, she will eventually." Sameer tried to instigate fear in Adi.

"Why are you saying this? You know I love her," Adi started to feel edgy.

"Both of you are mature individuals. If it doesn't work out, both of you will have to move on. But due to the fear of drowning, if you do not jump in the pool, you will never learn how to swim. So go ahead."

"Are you sure?"

"I am, if you are, about Natalie."

"Yes, I am," Adi said in excitement.

Again, Adi stared at the beer and took a long pause, his mind racing but not able to comprehend the implications of what he had just said.

Adi was as nerdy as Sameer when it came to romance and relationships. He broke the silence with

"Go ahead, means, what should I do exactly?"

"Go ahead and propose to her to marry you."

"PROPOSE!" Adi exclaimed.

"No, no, no. I cannot do that. I am not ready. It's too early," Adi panicked.

The reaction was expected. Sameer tried to convince Adi for some time as per the points that were tutored to him by Malini. Adi did not agree.

"Also, what if she is not ready? What if she says no? I can't risk that."

"So, you do want to get married to her but are scared that she would say no."

"No. I mean, yes, I guess. I don't know."

The YES in the sentence sandwiched between NO and I GUESS was a big step. It was tactfully brought out of Adi's inner conscience without feeling pressurized or cornered, which would have turned things for the worse.

"Okay, let us take baby steps. She wants you to meet her parents. She is ready for that. Let's do that first. Can we do that?"

"Yes."

"Then go ahead and suggest that to her before she asks for it. If it comes from you, it will mean more to her."

"Yes."

It all made sense to him, but Adi's mind was still catching up on what had happened over the past half an hour or so. He could only muster a "Yes" to Sameer's suggestion.

Sameer was relieved and proud of his achievement. He couldn't wait to go back and tell Malini how well he had done.

The Train Ride

Two weekends later, Adi and Natalie were on a train to visit Natalie's parents. It was a day trip, and they planned to return the same day. They took an early morning train.

Adi was a little nervous, though convinced that he was doing the right thing. Natalie was nervous herself, though happy that Adi suggested meeting with her parents by himself without her asking him again to do so. Natalie was nervous because of her mother. She was not in favor of having a non-German son-in-law. She realized that she was thinking ahead of time. This visit was just to introduce her boyfriend to her parents, nothing more.

Adi and Natalie reached Natalie's parents' place at around 11 a.m. As Natalie rings the doorbell, she whispers to Adi.

"Okay, babe, just be yourself. My parents are really cool."

"Got it. Be myself. Easy," Adi replied nervously. Adi was sweating.

Bernhard opened the door and welcomed them to the living room.

"Where's Ma?"

"She's upstairs."

"I'll go get her." Natalie rushed upstairs, leaving Adi with Bernhard. She was comfortable with her dad; he was cool. It was her mum she was worried about.

Marie was already grumpy about Adi's non-German origins.

"Who comes at 11 a.m.? It's neither breakfast nor evening teatime. Who comes for the first meeting for lunch?"

"Ma, be nice to him and no comments on being Indian or non-German."

Bernhard and Adi downstairs were already hitting it off.

"Nice to meet you, Mr. Schmidt."

"Adi, nice to finally meet you. Natalie talks about you all the time."

"Hopefully, only good stuff."

"Oh, Natalie has said you are quite a catch."

"Well, nice to hear that. All I hear from her is how I fall short of her expectations as a boyfriend," Adi chuckled nervously.

"Get used to it, son, get used to it. It only gets worse," Bernhard responded, laughing loudly. Adi realized he was hinting at marriage. It was a joke. Adi did not mind.

Adi's nervousness started to disappear gradually.

"What do you do for a living, son? Of course, Natalie has told us you do something in IT."

"Oh, I do not work in IT for sure. I am a data scientist for a marketing firm. I enable them to come up with strategies to increase sales."

"That makes sense. I tell you, for these mass communication and media people, everything is IT."

"I've tried to explain what I do a few times. It's just beyond her."

Natalie heard that as she and Marie were climbing down the stairs.

"Already gossiping about me? I can understand they think I am spoiled, good for nothing," Natalie said, pointing at her parents.

"Adi, I didn't expect that from you." Everyone had a nice laugh at that.

Adi felt it was a good start. His nervousness disappeared completely. The group talked about various topics for the next hour. Marie's participation was scarce, though she maintained basic courtesy to treat and behave well with the invited guest. Also, Natalie had warned her about the non-German topic. It was time for lunch.

"Let me get the lunch going."

"I will help you, Ma."

Bernhard was waiting for some alone time with Adi. As the women walked out of the living room, Bernhard offered Adi to show his book collection in the study room. Both walked to the study room.

Bernhard had a wall-to-wall shelf filled with books. It was an impressive collection. An avid reader would know. Adi wasn't.

"Wow, you have quite a collection," Adi pretended to like it and praised the collection to earn some brownie points from Bernhard.

"Thank you. Do you read much?"

"Yes," Adi hesitated, then continued.

"Actually, no. I am not much of a reader. I do read. Very rarely. I have read a few books. I read if I have nothing else left to do, which is never." Adi realized he was starting to rant and stopped.

Bernhard smiled.

"Son," Bernhard paused for a moment. He came close to Adi, looked him in the eye, put on a grim expression on his face, and continued with a whisper and terror in his tone.

"Take care of her. Take good care of her. If you ever so much as bring a tear to her eyes, I will make sure you cry for the rest of your life. You will be finished."

Bernhard paused and continued to stare into Adi's eyes. Adi stood there in shock, staring back.

About five seconds passed, and then Bernhard burst into laughter.

"I always wanted to do this," Bernhard continued, laughing.

"I am sorry, son."

Adi was still in shock and could only muster, "Is it?" with a nervous smile.

After a while, as his laugh subsided, Bernhard started speaking in the soft, sincere voice of a caring father.

"No. Seriously. I wanted to tell you this. She is a wonderful young girl. She is so loving, and she really cares for people whom she holds dear. And you are one of them. She loves you dearly. Appreciate what you have."

Bernhard took a few steps toward the door of the study room and continued after a pause.

"I do not know what you and Natalie have planned for the future, and it is totally up to both of you. But whoever gets to spend his life with her will be a lucky man."

Adi could feel a father's pride, sincere care, and affection for his daughter at that moment.

"I understand, Sir."

"Come on now, we are getting late for lunch," Bernhard waved his hand to call Adi and snapped out of the moment before it got too emotional for him.

While Adi was having his conversation with Bernhard, Sameer was struggling to meet the expectations of his work and home responsibilities. It was a day when he thought even two Sameers wouldn't be enough to meet everyones expectations of him. Malini had some urgent chores to run and visit the older child's school for a PTM. So the responsibility of household chores and taking care of their toddler Diya fell upon Sameer during the first half of the day. It was an unusually busy day at work with back-to-back meetings. Sameer had to work from home and take meetings online. In all the chaos Sameer forgot to start the laundry. Later, while juggling between the laptop and the preparation of their toddler's food during an ongoing online call, he did not fasten the mixer grinder's lid tightly before running it. It was a disaster. There was porridge all across the kitchen walls, floor, refrigerator, and his laptop. Fortunately his laptop was still working in spite of being drenched in porridge.

Despite the disaster, Sameer unmuted the call and continued working as it was on an important online call with his client. Sameer thought he would clean up the mess in half an hour after the call. Meanwhile, Diya was hungry, and she started crying. Sameer achieved new heights of multitasking that day. In between muting and unmuting the call while walking and going to the kitchen to calm down Diya and rushing away to another room so that Diya's crying is not heard on the call, somehow Sameer tried to focus on what was being discussed on the call and answer the questions he was asked.

Sameer had hoped Malini did not witness this. However, to his bad luck, Malini returned while this chaos was in progress. Malini witnessed that the kitchen was a complete mess; their daughter was hungry and crying, laundry was not done, and her husband was busy talking on the call.

Sameer felt he was doing everything he could to help and support the family, while Malini felt he was too busy with his work and friends and not paying enough attention to the family. Sameer and Malini ended up in a big fight unaware of the transformation that Adi was going through.

"She is a wonderful young girl. She is so loving and really cares for people who she holds dear to her. And you are one of them. She loves you dearly. Appreciate what you have."

These words from Bernhard flipped a switch in Adi's heart.

At times, things are in front of you, but you need somebody to point them out to you for you to notice them. Adi always knew Natalie loved him dearly, the way she looked at him, cared for him, and wanted to be with him.

Adi was not sure, though, why his mind and heart were so cluttered and confused about it so far. When he heard Bernhard say how much Natalie loved her, everything became clear in his mind and heart.

Those words coming from Natalie's father, who would have the best interest of Natalie in his mind, subconsciously had a bigger impact on Adi. He experienced a newfound deep love and connection for Natalie.

He kept stealing a glance at Natalie as they had lunch while continuing to engage in conversation with her parents. Adi was feeling immense love for Natalie, unable to take his eyes off her. Natalie could sense Adi's loving stare and was pleasantly surprised by the attention she was getting.

She could feel the love and childlike excitement for her in Adi's eyes. It almost felt like the time when they first fell in love. Natalie was surprised and not sure what caused this sudden change in Adi. She was not complaining. She was loving it, though she was getting a little conscious and worried that her parents would notice this romance that was going on in front of them.

As they concluded the lunch and Natalie's parents left the room for a bit, "What happened to you, what's going on?"

"Nothing. I love you," Adi said and moved to the living room. Natalie and Bernhard joined him for a while. Marie followed with coffee for everyone.

The group had become comfortable with each other by this time. Even Natalie's mother liked Adi's company, though the German factor remained. As they sat there having coffee and chatting, Adi stole a glance at her. He noticed Natalie was staring at him. She maintained her stare as Adi looked at her. Usually, Adi would get very conscious of this and look away, especially in the presence of others. Natalie maintained the gaze, assuming he would look away this time as well. Adi did not. He kept looking into her eyes with a loving stare. A few moments passed. Bernhard noticed the duel between them while Marie was busy reading a pastry recipe in the magazine they were talking about. Apparently, Marie had adored Adi's interest in cooking and baking, something her daughter never liked.

Bernhard cleared his throat loudly, breaking the duel. Natalie looked away, wondering what had gotten into Adi. She smiled to herself, feeling good about all the attention she was getting from Adi.

As the evening approached, Adi and Natalie left to return to Berlin. On their way back to the train station, in the cab, Natalie inquired about the day and her parents. She was happy to hear Adi's positive response about the day and even more excited to hear how much Adi liked her parents. That meant a lot to her. She would call her parents later to get their feedback and hoped they enjoyed the day and loved Adi as well.

It was a long day, and both were tired. They sat quietly as the train raced toward Berlin. The railway compartment they were in was almost empty, with very few passengers. Adi was on a window seat, and Natalie sat beside him.

Natalie was feeling blissful with the events of the day. It was a big day; her boyfriend met her parents for the first time, and they liked each other. Even her mother. To top it all, Adi's attention and love for her made her day even more special. Natalie placed her arm around his arm, rested her head on Adi's shoulder, and closed her eyes, reminiscing the day's events. Adi tilted his head, resting it delicately on hers. She felt safe and relaxed in his arms.

Adi was ecstatic and reminisced about the day and the happy times he had spent with Natalie. Adi recollected his first meeting with her, the time when he expressed his love for her, their trekking tours, breakfast outings, and many more instances. All of it brought a smile to his face.

"I am a lucky man to have her," Adi thought to himself.

As he thought this, Bernhard's words filled his mind.

"Whoever gets to spend his life with her will be a lucky man."

"Natalie," Adi whispered softly.

"Ya"

"Are you asleep?"

"No, why?"

Love was in the air as they nestled together, basking in the warmth of each other's presence and the joy of the day's events. Their delicate whispers were their own that no one else could hear.

"I want to tell you something," Natalie's head was still resting on his shoulder, and her arm around his arm.

"Go ahead."

Adi took her hand in his and caressed it.

"Marry me," Adi whispered.

Natalie was excited and did not expect it. However, Natalie did not react.

"Are you sure?" Natalie responded softly after a few seconds without opening her eyes.

"Yes, I am. I want to marry you."

"Okay, good. Then plan well, prepare for it, and propose to me properly."

"Ok."

The proposal was romantic but lacked the pomp and pageantry that Natalie dreamed of. Adi understood that Natalie's response meant yes, but his proposal didn't meet her expectations.

Both traveled silently, cherishing each other's company without speaking for the rest of their journey.

Sameer got off the phone with Adi that evening. It was late after dinner. Malini walked out of the kids' bedroom, a little annoyed that Sameer had been glued to the phone for the past half an hour. She had to put the kids to sleep, and it was Sameer's job.

"You won't believe what happened."

"I am not interested. You could have talked to whoever it was you were talking to after putting the kids to sleep," It was a weeknight, and Malini was tired of the day's struggles. In addition to that Sameer was not at all helpful all day. Malini went to their bedroom, irritated. Sameer followed.

"It was Adi. You will forget all your irritation if you know what Adi did."

Malini got a little curious but continued getting ready for bed, still irritated. Sameer waited until he had her attention.

"What?" she couldn't stop her curiosity after a while.

"And you were criticizing me for what I did. You thought I would mess things up. But see the impact of what I did. You should be proud of me," Sameer wanted to take the credit for what Adi had just told him over the phone.

"Do not irritate me further, Sameer. I am tired. Tell me if you want to or don't bother."

"Adi proposed to Natalie."

"What?" Malini exclaimed.

"How, when, where. He was not even ready to meet her parents casually, and suddenly this."

"That's the effect of my advice to him the other day at Mizo's. You thought it was no good. But that changed his mind."

"Yeah, right. Good job, Sameer. I am proud of you," Malini retorted in a sarcastic tone.

"Stop basking in self-glory and tell me everything."

It was past 2 a.m. Revathi's phone rang.

Harpreet was a light sleeper and an early riser too. He could not sleep beyond 6 a.m., no matter how late he slept, and was often unable to complete his sleep because of this. He needed to sleep in the afternoon on weekends to complete his sleep deficit, a topic of argument with Revathi as she felt he spoiled the weekend sleeping. Unlike Harpreet, Revathi was blessed with good sound sleep. She could sleep through a noisy circus and could sleep till late in the morning.

The phone ring interrupted Harpreet's sleep while Revathi continued to sleep. Irritated at this odd-hour phone call and with Revathi showing no signs of receiving the call, Harpreet reached out to the phone. It was from Malini. A sudden fear gripped Harpreet. "Was everything fine? Did something happen to Adi?" Ill thoughts crossed his mind momentarily. He immediately shook Revathi to wake her up before receiving the call.

"Wake up, it's Malini calling. I wonder what it is."

"Hello, Malini. Is everything okay?"

"Namaste, Tayaji. Is Taiji around?" Malini started with greetings before inquiring about Revathi.

"Of course, she is here," Harpreet snapped in irritation. "What's wrong? Is everything ok?"

"Yes. Everything is fine. I just wanted to update Taiji on something."

"Update Taiji on something? Do you know what time it is? Couldn't you..." Revathi snatched the phone from Harpreet before he could complete the sentence.

Harpreet was irritated by this odd-hour call when there was no emergency. He had an important day at the office tomorrow.

"Couldn't she have waited until morning?"

He stared back at Revathi in irritation and surprise, wondering what update couldn't wait until morning.

"Don't worry, you go back to sleep," Revathi shrugged him off as she wanted to hear what update Malini had on Adi's visit to Natalie's parents.

Revathi got out of bed, phone to her ear, and walked toward the bedroom door.

"Tell me what the update is."

"What update?" Harpreet said, getting up from the bed to follow Revathi to the living room.

"This will take a while; you go back to bed," Revathi said. She walked out of the bedroom, leaving Harpreet, who was already irritated and furious that she had left him in the dark about the update.

Harpreet had no choice but to try to sleep. He was sure sleep would deceive him.

It was about 40 minutes before Revathi came back. Harpreet was still awake. Revathi updated Harpreet on all that had transpired in Adi's life: the visit to Natalie's parents and the proposal.

"Get ready for a German daughter-in-law," Revathi was beaming with happiness.

"I am happy for Adi if he really wants this," Harpreet said. She was disappointed at Harpreet's lukewarm response. Harpreet paused for a moment and then continued.

"I would still like to say stop interfering in his life. You know what happened when we got involved."

"Stop worrying, darling. Everything is fine. Learn to relax a bit."

Both decided not to discuss further to avoid an argument in the middle of the night.

The Innocent Secret

"Sameer, I do not know what to do. She is mad, we fought, it's over. I do not want it to be over," Adi sounded anxious.

Sameer was Adi's go-to friend. Always talking and sharing their lives with each other. Adi being the emotional, aspirational, and dramatic type, often landed in difficult situations.

"I am not getting a word you are saying."

Knowing Adi for several years, Sameer was familiar with the anxious nervousness that he sensed in Adi's voice whenever he was in some trouble. Adi continued his ranting about Natalie and his mother. Sameer could not understand anything.

"Calm down, let's meet at Mizo's in 30 minutes."

They were at Mizo's, their usual hangout in 30 minutes. They ordered a beer, which was served promptly. Adi gulped half a pint in one go. Sameer experienced a déjà vu moment.

After returning from Turkey, life was going wonderfully for Natalie. However, a constant fear bothered Adi. He had no way out but to confront the problem and tell Natalie about who his mother was. Sameer also advised him to do so. Adi never mustered the courage to do so. He was very aware of the idealistic thinking of Natalie, "We have to be honest and transparent with each other."

It was a Friday evening. Natalie and Adi had planned to go out for dinner. Adi had some online office meetings that he planned to attend from home. To save time, they decided to meet at Adi's place so that they could leave as soon as Adi finished his meeting. Natalie finished her work and left for Adi's house at 6.30 p.m. It was a short 15-minute subway ride. She was at Adi's place before 7 p.m. She rang the doorbell. Adi opened the door carrying his laptop in hand. His meeting was in progress. He gestured to Natalie to come in and signaled five minutes with his fingers two, three, or maybe four times. The exact time could be anyone's guess from the way he signaled. Natalie assumed 10 minutes but knew it could be longer based on her experience. As always, later, they would end up arguing about what Adi had signaled and the exact time he said. Whenever Natalie used to get irritated with delays due to Adi's meetings, Adi used to joke that his meetings were like his girlfriend getting ready for a party. Ten minutes could mean half an hour.

Natalie waited in the living room while Adi was finishing his meeting in the bedroom. She sat on the couch, scrolling through her phone. Bored of it, she kept her phone aside. She noticed her magazine on the coffee table that she had forgotten earlier. Natalie leaned forward to take the magazine when an envelope fell from the coffee table. As Natalie leaned further to pick up the envelope, she noticed something written on it.

From: Dr. Revathi Iyengar
Mumbai, India.

Natalie was surprised to see that. She was intrigued; why was there a letter from Dr. Revathi to Adi? Principled as she was, Natalie did not open the envelope to read its content. However, she was very curious and wondered what business Dr. Revathi would have with Adi. Why had Adi never mentioned that he knew Dr. Revathi when she had been going on and on about her meeting with Dr. Revathi in Turkey? Rather, she had been talking about Dr. Revathi long before her trip to Turkey when she had started reading Dr. Revathi's book. Natalie was impatient by nature, which made her too curious to wait for Adi's meeting to end. She grabbed the envelope in her hand and walked straight to the bedroom to inquire about it. Natalie held the envelope high in front of Adi so that he could see it. She was considerate enough to wait for him to mute his microphone on the call before she spoke. However, she wasn't patient enough to wait until his meeting ended. She expected Adi to be available and prioritize her over his work, which was a hard ask at times while Adi was in the middle of an important meeting.

Adi's heart skipped a beat, seeing the letter from his mother in Natalie's hand. He was distracted from the call when someone on the call asked a question to Adi. Adi recovered from the shock and somehow answered the question. Natalie was still there waiting for Adi to mute the microphone so that she could talk to Adi. Realizing Natalie would not relent and the meeting would not end quickly, Adi pretended to have a bad network connection and disconnected the call.

"I can explain. She is my mother." Natalie was shocked to hear that.

"I was going to tell you, but I forgot."

"You forgot who your mother was."

"No, I mean, I wanted to tell, but…"

"You hid such important information while I had been telling you for so long to introduce me to your parents."

Adi was scared. Adi had seen Natalie angry several times over their small and big differences. But this was different. This was serious.

"You did not even tell me when I went on and on about meeting Dr. Revathi."

"No, I wanted to tell you, but…"

"But what? You were having fun with me. Were you enjoying it, keeping the truth about your mother from me?"

"No. I was worried. I was scared. Scared of this outburst. You tend to be too dramatic, and you keep getting angry at small things, and you always want things your way."

Fights in relationships often lose their focus on the subject. The parties involved in the fight turn it into personal disputes, and emotions run high. Winning the argument takes precedence over addressing the initial issue that caused the fight in the first place. History books on past conflicts are referred to, and every failure of each other is quoted. Obviously, there is a difference of opinion on facts and how things happened in the historical disputes, adding more fuel to the fight. Sometimes, facts are distorted and exaggerated to create a more dramatic impact to win the argument. Adding ego to the mix creates a concoction that can generate a fight of epic proportions.

Natalie and Adi's fight followed all these standard traits of a fight.

"Is that so? If I am so bad, why don't you leave me?"

Experts say to have a productive fight, it's crucial to stay composed, listen actively, and keep the conversation restricted to the issue at hand. Natalie and Adi did exactly the opposite.

They lost their cool, got personal, and let their egos drive the conversation. Natalie was emotionally hurt.

"I do not want to talk to you. But I will tell you this: you have really hurt me," she said. She walked away. This is something Natalie said after every fight, and then later, they would reconcile. Adi knew this fight was much deeper and more serious.

Natalie was hurt. As she lay in bed that night, heartbroken, her mind kept building up the gravity of the deceit that Adi had woven. She remembered numerous occasions when she had talked about Dr. Revathi to Adi, but he had not once mentioned the simple fact that Dr. Revathi was his mother. When she went to Turkey and met Dr. Revathi for the first time, Natalie had been talking on and on about her meeting with Dr. Revathi. She even borrowed the book Dr. Revathi had written from Adi. Suddenly, Natalie felt very stupid. She should have suspected something when she found Dr. Revathi's book about love and psychology with Adi. Adi was not a reader, and that was a book about love and psychology. She should have seen that something was out of place. With every such occasion that Natalie thought of, she felt more and more cheated.

Dr. Revathi had visited Berlin. She remembered how Adi had prevented her from visiting his place and meeting her during that period. The thought of Adi's mother being in town for so long, right there in Berlin, and he never bothered to introduce her to his mother made her furious. She screamed and threw the pillow against the wall to release her frustration.

Natalie's heart sank as she realized the extent of Adi's deceit. She had trusted him and confided in him, only to be met with falsehoods and manipulation. All this when Adi knew she had been asking Adi to meet his parents. At that moment, she felt a profound sense of loss, as if the foundation of their relationship had crumbled beneath her feet.

For Natalie, honesty was the cornerstone of any meaningful relationship. Without it, their love had no meaning. By the book, the idealistic personality that Natalie had was probably making the gravity of the situation more severe than what it really was. With a heavy heart, Natalie realized that she could no longer trust Adi. She even felt Adi's love and the proposal were all a façade and a lie.

Adi's anger from the argument with Natalie over his lie subsided, and he felt deep remorse for what had happened. He wished he had told her about his mother the first time Natalie talked about Dr. Revathi. But what's past cannot be changed. He wished, only if Natalie would understand that he did not mean anything wrong and hoped she understood what he did was unintentional and driven by his own insecurities and nature. Through the night, Adi's mind took him on a guilt trip. He developed the feeling of remorse and a wish to mend things with Natalie. However, through the same night, Natalie's mind did exactly the opposite. She felt cheated, her anger for Adi multiplied, and she emotionally distanced herself from Adi.

Adi tried to reach out to Natalie the next day to apologize. But Natalie had cut him off, severing all ties with him. She closed the door to any possibility of reconciliation, refusing to meet him or even talk to him on the phone. Each attempt by Adi to talk to her was met with cold indifference. With each unanswered call and unsuccessful meeting attempt, Adi realized the gravity of the situation. Repairing the damage he had caused was not going to be easy.

Two weeks later, Adi's patience was wearing thin. The rigor with which he tried to get through to Natalie was also diminishing. He started feeling resentment toward Natalie.

"It's not that big a crime that I committed that she is not even talking to me," he thought to himself. Probably he was right to some extent. The view may vary depending on who you ask.

The fear of losing Natalie made him carry on with trying to talk to her. He was fighting his ego with every rejection and persisting with it. Adi himself did not know how long he would be able to fight and win over his ego. The day his ego won over him, he would stop trying. Few realize ego is the death knell of most broken relationships.

After days of pursuing and numerous voice messages, Natalie replied and agreed to meet him. They met at Monbijou park. Natalie did not want to meet at home or in a café. It was a nice, sunny day, and the park was full of people who had visited the park to enjoy the lovely weather. They found an isolated spot at the riverfront on the bank of the Spree River in the park.

"Tell me what you want to talk about."

"I am sorry."

"Does a sorry make everything fine? You broke my heart. You lied."

"I said I am sorry. That's why I have been trying to reach out to you for the last two weeks."

"You should, you made a mistake. But I will not forgive you."

One of the key mantras for diffusing the risk in a relationship is overcoming personal idealism. Idealism is an unrealistic belief that ideals should be pursued at all costs. Humans are complex beings. Their beliefs, conduct, and emotions are crafted by their natural physiological construct, especially that of the brain, and experiential overprint on it as they live through their life. No two people have these identical. Certainly not for people from opposite genders. Add to that the several layers of emotions that are involved in relationships. The concoction becomes even more potent for disaster. There is no room for personal idealism in this equation if relationships were to work. Natalie had read this in Dr. Revathi's book and agreed with the thought. But she never realized she was making the mistake that was pointed out in the book.

In simple words, it means nobody is perfect, and the definition of perfection differs from person to person. One should be ready to accept a partner's imperfections in a relationship. How much imperfection is acceptable is a personal choice?

"You think this is not a big issue. I thought you were sorry for what you did."

"That is what I said first thing when I came here. I am sorry. You are going round and round on this," Adi was running out of patience. He got angry. She was already angry. That was the end of any sensible conversation. Again, weapons of words were hurled at each other, past incidences were brought forth, mistakes were recounted, and each other's behavioral deficiencies were highlighted. It was a massacre on both sides.

At one point, Natalie stopped. "I can't deal with this. You have hurt me so badly with all the things that you have said and done." She turned around and walked away.

Adi was frustrated as Natalie was not ready to let go and forgive. Adi did not follow suit. The meeting did not turn out the way he was expecting it to be.

All Hell Breaks Loose!

Adi was feeling very low as he sat alone at home after the big fight with Natalie. The perfect proposal that he made to Natalie just a week before played in his mind.

It was exactly a week back that he and Natalie walked hand in hand with Adi along the picturesque walkway on the cliff overlooking the lake below along the hiking trail.

Adi had planned an evening excursion along the lake, an hour's drive from Berlin. He had scouted several locations and picked this one for its perfect view and ambiance in the evening.

As they reached a beautiful clearing in the forest by the lake, the sun was about to set. It painted the sky in shades of pink and gold. The air was filled with the fragrance of blooming flowers.

Natalie loved the sunsets, and it was the perfect spot. Earlier that week, Adi had visited the exact spot and waited an entire evening to time the sunset.

Taking a deep breath, Adi faced Natalie, his eyes filled with sincerity. "Natalie, from the moment we met, I knew you were the one. You make my every day brighter, my every moment special. I can't imagine my life without you. I love you more than words can say."

Natalie's heart skipped a beat as she realized this was the moment she had been waiting for. She stood there facing Adi as he reached into his pocket to pull out the ring. Seeing this, Natalie's eyes widened; her lips parted in sheer surprise. Overwhelmed by the moment, she instinctively covered her mouth with both hands. A burst of excitement surged through her, and she began to bounce gently on the balls of her feet, the anticipation and joy manifesting in a rhythmic, elated dance.

The elation was short-lived. Adi fumbled and dropped the ring box. The ring parted from the box, rolled gently, and fell across the lake fence into the lake 20 feet below. Adi and Natalie watched this happen in disbelief.

Natalie saw her proposal diving into the lake. She was in shock. "Adi!" Natalie exclaimed, her voice a mixture of surprise and concern. She instinctively looked down at the water, her mind racing with the realization that the symbol of their love was now submerged in the deep lake.

Natalie, torn between laughter and disbelief, couldn't help but break into a nervous giggle.

"You really know how to make it memorable, don't you?"

She kept leaning over the fence, hoping to see the ring box floating in the orange glimmer of the setting sun.

"Natalie," he called out, his voice low and filled with a mix of nerves and excitement.

She turned around, her expression a blend of surprise and curiosity. The sight that greeted her took her breath away—there was Adi, on his knee, a genuine and nervous smile playing on his lips. In his hands, he held the ring, the sunlight catching the glimmering diamond.

"Natalie," he continued, his eyes locked with hers, "I may have dropped an empty box, but what I'm holding now is the real deal. Will you make me the happiest person in the world and marry me?"

Natalie's eyes widened in disbelief, a mix of emotions playing on her face. She gasped, covering her mouth with both hands, and her eyes welled up with tears of joy. The surprise and the genuine moment unfolded in a way that, despite the initial confusion, made the proposal even more unforgettable. He slipped the ring onto her finger. With the ring securely on Natalie's finger, Adi stood up and gave her a warm, tight hug. Natalie, still caught in the multitude of emotional ups and downs over the past few minutes, reciprocated with a tight embrace feeling safe in Adi's arms. They shared a sweet, tender moment, sealing their promise with a kiss.

However, as they pulled back from the hug, Natalie couldn't help but playfully hit Adi on the chest. "You almost had me in tears there with the box trick. Don't you ever do such things to me." Both laughed.

They sat there on the bench holding each other's hands, watching the sun set in the lake. As darkness settled in, they remained on the bench, not in a hurry to break the spell of the moment. Wrapped in the warmth of each other's presence, they felt a deep gratitude for finding each other's love.

Adi could not bear the sudden drop from bliss to misery in their relationship and needed to talk to someone. He summoned Sameer for a drink and sensing the seriousness in Adi's voice, Sameer obliged. He was risking a major bashing from Malini as it was a weekday, but his friend needed him. Also, Malini would understand as she was also too invested in the matchmaking of Adi and Natalie.

Adi narrated the events over the past two weeks.

"I told you, don't lie, tell her the truth."

"When did you say that? And what do you mean by lying? It's not like I lied. I just did not tell who my mum was."

"Ya. Right."

"I don't know what to do. She is not talking to me. I've been trying for the last two weeks."

"It looks serious. She has taken it too seriously. Your lies."

"One last time, Sameer. Stop saying that. I did not lie, just did not tell the truth," Adi reacted frustrated. He was clueless on what's to be done next.

"The only good part of all of this was that I never introduced Natalie to Amma. Unnecessarily they would get worried if they knew that things were not working out between me and Natalie. Especially after all that had happened earlier with Rashi."

Sameer began to say something and then stopped. Sameer wasn't sure what to do. He hesitated. Adi sensed there was something wrong, seeing his reaction.

"What are you not telling me? What are you hiding? Do they know?"

"Actually, they do," Sameer hesitantly nodded his head with a concerned, scared look on his face, not sure how Adi would react.

"Great. Thank you. And you call me your friend. Why did you tell them? It was our secret. I told you because you are my friend. You are not supposed to tell this to anyone else. Come on." Adi ranted in frustration for a while.

Sameer's friendship was being questioned, which he could not sit and accept. He spilled the beans.

"It was not me. I did not tell anyone. They already knew. Taiji and Tayaji. Even before she visited Germany."

"What? How?"

"Nothing."

"Sameer, you have to tell me everything now."

Sameer was in a pickle. He ended up telling everything to Adi. Adi and Natalie's telltale through a TV show and video call, Revathi's travel to Turkey and then Germany, scheming and spying with the help of Malini and making him a tool in all of this. Adi couldn't believe what he was hearing.

Sameer messed up first by telling Revathi that he knew about it. Saying that they knew even before Revathi was in Germany and the whole story behind it was a disaster. He was going to be in the line of fire from both Adi and Malini for this. Adi was disappointed that Sameer was part of it and that he never told Adi about what was going on.

Sameer knew that he could manage his friend's disappointment. The bigger problem was Malini. He was scared and not sure how he would face Malini when she found out that he spilled the beans to Adi. He would get an earful from Malini. The thought itself sent chills down his spine.

Both sat there silently, trying to make sense of what had happened. Adi was in shock and angry, while Sameer was contemplating the depth of trouble he was in after telling everything to Adi. Adi broke the silence after several minutes.

"Why do they meddle with my life? Last time as well, they messed up everything. They are doing it again."

"Adi. This is wrong and you know it. Whatever happened with Rashi was not her fault. And it is not her fault this time as well. Taiji only wanted to help."

Adi said not-so-polite things to Sameer, and it turned into a fight. Eventually, dejected and disappointed at the closest people in his life, he quietly got up and left without speaking a word.

The day had started with a sweet hope for Adi that he would mend things with Natalie after the meeting. Natalie wouldn't admit it to herself, but she also hoped in the morning that things mended with Adi. By the end of the day, everything had turned bitter and against their expectations. Frustration, anger, and resentment were the flavor of the evening. Adi was frustrated and angry at Natalie. Natalie was hurt and disappointed in Adi. They were close to the end of their love story. Adi felt deceived and was angry at Revathi as well. He had the worst fight ever with his best friend and was angry at Sameer as well and Sameer was hurt and sad for all the mean things that Adi said to Sameer.

Knowing about the mess, Malini was angry with Sameer. They had a big fight; tempers flared, doors got slammed, and Sameer ended up on his couch. Both were no longer on speaking terms that evening and for a few days to come.

Since it was a serious matter, Malini called up Revathi to inform her of what had happened. It was late in India. Hesitantly, Revathi passed on the update to Harpreet. Harpreet uttered, "I told you not to meddle in Adi's life." That comment flared up an argument between the two, which advanced into a full-fledged fight. They ended up sleeping, turning their backs toward each other.

It was a sleepless night for all of them.

The next morning, Revathi tried calling Adi. However, Adi did not want to talk to Revathi. He was making the same mistake that Natalie did, cutting off the communication. Momentarily, it was fine, even helpful when one is angry, to avoid escalation. However, a prolonged cutoff is what Adi also did. Adi cut off from everyone. He stopped taking Revathi's calls and even avoided Sameer when he tried to reach out on Revathi's request.

Several weeks passed.

Reminiscing about the period of his romance with Natalie and the events that led up to his proposal to Natalie, Adi felt it was all a deception created by Revathi and her troop. He started doubting whether he ever loved Natalie for real. A stupid thought, as he was clearly unhappy being away from Natalie. But who could correct him? He was not talking to anyone.

Natalie was also unhappy being away from Adi. The anger over Adi's lies had subsided, and somewhere inside her, she hoped Adi would call her or meet her. He did not, and her ego stopped her from reaching out to him.

Was it Really Love

"Adi, wake up. I will be sending some laborers to take this furniture out to your aunt's place this afternoon. So be at home," Harpreet instructed Adi.

It had been four days since he had returned to India, and he had adjusted to the Indian time. He still slept until 10 a.m., but that was just a relaxed vacation schedule and not jet lag. Revathi did not mind it as he was back in India on vacation after five years. Revathi also realized that Adi was still hurting and might not be sleeping well at night due to that.

Earlier, while Adi was still in school and college, Revathi never allowed this.

Several weeks had passed since the sleepless night that kept everyone involved awake and restless. Time heals everything. Things got better as the time passed. The hurt and the pain of separation with Natalie reduced, though it still troubled Adi. He still loved her.

As time passed, things got better between Adi and Revathi as well. He spent several days avoiding Revathi's calls. Efforts from Sameer to talk to him were also declined by Adi. Eventually, he gave in and answered Revathi's call.

The conversation wasn't pleasant. Adi blamed Revathi for spoiling things between Natalie and him. Adi vented all his frustrations by blaming everything on Revathi. Revathi calmly listened to him without defending herself. Adi knew in his heart it was not Revathi's fault, neither in the current mess with Natalie nor in his breakup with Rashi. Once his venting lost steam, he calmed down.

"Amma, I am sorry."

"It's okay, Kanna," Revathi called Adi *Kanna* endearingly in Tamil.

Adi was in tears. Though not on a video call, his voice gave away that he was crying.

"I didn't mean for any of this to happen. I loved her," he paused for a moment. Revathi sensed that separation from Natalie was hurting Adi more than anything. He loved her dearly.

"If you love her, go and talk to her. Mend things with her."

"Absolutely not. Not anymore. I tried and tried for a very long time. She is being unreasonable. And I am not sure now if I even loved her and wanted to marry her in the first place."

Revathi realized Adi was referring to her meddling in making him propose to Natalie. She kept quiet and did not respond. Revathi knew she was not responsible for the reason why they fought, but she did nudge him a little into proposing. Revathi wouldn't call it meddling. It was just a little nudge, which she believed was needed.

Revathi knew Adi was hurting and wanted to be there for him.

"Why don't you come to India for some time? You will feel better."

"Let me think about it."

Adi needed that change. Adi agreed to visit India on the condition that no one would talk about Natalie.

Two weeks later, Adi was in India.

After Harpreet instructed Adi about the furniture movement, Revathi and Harpreet went to work while Adi spent a lazy morning sitting at home reminiscing moments with Natalie.

In the afternoon, two laborers came to move the furniture. Adi supervised the movement and ensured that no damage was done to the furniture while it was being moved down three flights of stairs and loaded onto the back of a truck.

Adi heard the two laborers talking to each other while they were moving the furniture.

"Why do you need the money?"

"My son has a wish, and tomorrow is his birthday. I want to gift him his wish."

"I wish I could help."

The words resonated with Adi.

"I wish I could help more," Natalie used to always say.

Those words took Adi back to Natalie's thoughts.

Natalie used to work at the community kitchen for the underprivileged and also used to donate a decent amount of money to them to feed the poor. Adi, not too keen on it, had accompanied her a few times to work along with her at the community kitchen. Adi remembered his conversation with Natalie.

"Why do you do this? Don't you wish to rest after your hectic week?" Adi had asked.

"I wish I could help more. It gives me happiness."

"And what's with the donations?"

"I have more than enough. If giving a little makes anyone's life better, then why not?"

"Sir, sir. We are done," Shivkumar broke Adi's train of thought.

Adi paid them what Harpreet had instructed him to pay.

"Sir, if you don't mind, do you have any other work that I can help you with? I need to earn some more money today. I need it. I will do anything."

Shivkumar was in need. Seeing this, Natalie's line echoed in his mind: "I have more than enough. If giving a little makes anyone's life better, then why not." Suffering from the separation from Natalie, the memory of Natalie's philanthropic work inspired Adi, and he was inclined to help Shivkumar. He knew Natalie would have done the same. Also, overhearing the laborers' conversation earlier, he realized it was for a good cause.

Adi invented a task that was not immediately necessary. He made Shivkumar switch Harpreet's car's tires from left to right and front to back. Typically, this is done so that tires wear evenly, but it was not absolutely necessary to be done then. Shivkumar had little experience doing the job, so Adi guided him through it. Adi paid Shivkumar handsomely for the work.

Adi felt happy and content doing a good deed, especially something that Natalie would have liked. He felt a little closer to Natalie than before.

Love, That Was

"I am going to have dinner today with Raghu."

"Okay. Then let us plan for our movie outing tomorrow. Where are you going for dinner?"

"At LocoMan's at the Eastend Mall."

It has been a couple of weeks since Adi's return. Revathi was happy Adi was socializing. He seemed back to his normal self.

Adi reached the Eastend Mall a little early as usual. His friend Raghu was a little late, again as usual. Instead of waiting at LocoMan's, he strolled around the mall. After about 20 minutes, Raghu called, saying he was parking his car and would be there at LocoMan's in 10 minutes. Adi started walking toward the restaurant. As he was about to enter the restaurant, he heard someone calling his name from behind. He turned around and, to his surprise, he saw Rashi waving her hand at him, looking more gorgeous and groomed than he remembered. She was a little too casual and disheveled earlier. She looked perfect now.

"Hey, what a surprise!" Rashi exclaimed as she walked toward Adi, a big smile beaming on her face.

"Wow. What a surprise."

"How come you went to Europe for an MBA, and I heard earlier from Rucha that you were working in Germany? Visiting parents?"

"Yes."

"Here for your wedding?"

"No. No. Long story."

Long story. Adi wondered why would he say that. Not that he wanted to share his current ex's story with his previous ex. Adi realized he was a little nervous and excited at the same time, seeing his first love after so many years.

"Oh, long story. Interesting. I would like to hear that."

Adi almost blushed.

"No, seriously. Let's catch up. How long have you been here in town?"

"Sure. I am here."

"I need to rush now, but I will call you."

They exchanged phone numbers, and Rashi rushed away.

Natalie had tried to distract herself by keeping herself busy at work. However, the hurt and pain of breaking up with Adi ceased to subside. She would lie in bed, awake all night, thinking about him. She cursed herself and regretted not giving Adi a chance every night. It was getting unbearable for Natalie, and she started blaming herself for it.

Unaware of Natalie's ordeal, Marie had called to invite Natalie to a get-together to celebrate the 30th anniversary of their wedding. No matter the differences, a child would feel at ease in a mother's comforting care like none other. The usually strong Natalie broke down in tears as she talked to her mother on the phone, which took Marie by surprise.

"Ma, I could have given him a chance. He tried. It's over now." Tears rolled down her cheeks as she spoke. She was gasping for breath. Realizing the seriousness of Natalie's state, Marie decided instantly.

"We are coming there to pick you up. You are coming here to stay with us for a few days."

Marie ordered Bernhard to be ready to drive down to Berlin early the next morning.

Back home, Natalie narrated the turn of events that happened over the past several weeks to Marie. No matter how close daughters are to their fathers, there are some things daughters would always prefer to talk to their mothers about. Mothers would understand their daughters' minds better.

Marie saw an opportunity to ensure that things ended with Adi forever by advising Natalie accordingly. However, seeing how deeply Natalie was in love with Adi, against her own preference, Marie consoled her and advised her to meet Adi and work things out with him.

"He has gone to India," Natalie informed Marie.

Hearing this, it appeared to Marie that things were beyond repair between Adi and Natalie. She felt sad for Natalie but also felt some happiness at the prospect of a non-German son-in-law appearing to fade.

Earlier, Sameer had tried to patch things up between Natalie and Adi. As Adi was being adamant and not trying to work things out with Natalie, he had advised Natalie to mend ways with Adi and stop him from going to India. However, she, too, had acted stubbornly and not reached out to Adi.

Rashi called up Adi the next day and they agreed to meet at a coffee shop, their old hangout place that was near her old residence.

"So, tell me how have you been."

"Well, doing well. I got married a year after we split. Of course, arranged, in a family of my parents' choice."

"Oh, okay," Adi sighed. Adi imagined Rashi in an old traditional household with a long ghoonghat (head scarf) covering her head and face.

"No. No. Don't give that reaction. It's a good thing. I got lucky. I have a loving husband. He and his family do not mind me working. He helps and supports me."

"Okay. Good. I am happy for you."

"I really got lucky. I am happy with my life. Of course, my parents played a big role in finding the right family for me."

"Of course," Adi felt happy that it all worked out well for Rashi.

Rashi narrated the whole story about her marriage and her life after marriage. It was all rosy. It made Adi a little jealous, and it was obvious that he was her ex-boyfriend, and she was talking with such fondness about her husband.

"Enough about me. What about you? What have you been up to?"

"Well, you know. MBA in the Netherlands. Then moved to Germany for a job."

"Yes, all that is fine. It's not a job interview. Tell me more. Is there someone special? Are you married? Girlfriend? Last I heard, you were still not married."

"Long story. Currently single."

Long story. Again. Adi wondered if he was fishing for sympathy from Rashi. But now he was caught.

"I have time. Go ahead. I shared everything with you. Now it's your turn."

Adi narrated his love story with Natalie.

"She is a tough one. She did not forgive you even after trying so much."

"Yes. What can I say? I always fall in love with all the difficult ones," Adi taunted Rashi. Both laughed.

"Let's take a walk in the old area."

"Sure."

Ten minutes later, both were on the dimly lit lanes around the building where Rashi used to stay. They had spent several evenings strolling these lanes.

"Tell me, Adi, do you still love this girl, Natalie?"

"It doesn't matter. It's past."

"While you were telling me your story, I could sense it. You still love her. Running away from it will not help Adi."

"Let it go, Rashi," Adi got a little annoyed.

Rashi decided not to push it.

Both silently walked slowly next to each other in the dimly lit lane, lost in their thoughts. Just like old times.

"You know, Adi, sometimes I wonder how it would be if we had gotten married." Adi was surprised to hear this, but he did not react.

"I feel it would have been wonderful. After all, you were my first love, my only love."

Adi was not sure what to say. He kept quiet.

"You know. You and I, husband and wife, living together. We were so comfortable with each other."

Adi was not sure where Rashi was going with this. He stopped, turned toward Rashi, and looked her in the eyes.

"Yes, I guess it would have been lovely. You and me."

Their gaze met, and they had a moment. A nostalgic moment of love and regret. It was the same spot where Adi had proposed to her.

"I wish you had tried a little harder. I wish you wouldn't have given up on us so soon."

"You wanted it to end."Rashi quietly stared into Adi's eyes on the dimly lit street. There was silence for several moments before she whispered softly.

"I did, but I wish you would have held on to us and convinced me out of it."

Adi felt a sharp pain of regret in his heart.

"You know, when one is having doubts and ready to give up, others must hold on to it and not give up. Only then will it last."

A car with its headlights on a high beam turned into the lane, breaking the moment. Rashi quickly snapped out of it and said, "Don't get me wrong. I am happy with my husband and my marriage. He is a very good man, and I love him dearly. I wouldn't change a thing about my current life." Rashi was telling the truth, though the "what if" thought about Adi sometimes crossed her mind.

"I guess we should turn back. Avinash is going to meet me at the mall. I don't want to be late."

They turned and started walking again toward her parked car. On their walk back, they were mostly silent except for some small talk.

Upon reaching Rashi's car, Adi said, "This is it. It was nice meeting you, Rashi."

"Yes, this is it," Rashi paused for a moment and then continued.

"You know, Adi, think about what I said earlier about not giving up. Maybe Natalie still wants you to reach out to her. Maybe you are giving up on your relationship with her too soon. We made that mistake earlier. Do not make that mistake again." Rashi paused as she looked straight into Adi's eyes. She could see a storm brewing inside Adi. She continued.

"I see that you still love her, and you know that it might work out with Natalie if you tried a little harder. You will regret it for the rest of your life if you don't give it a chance."

Rashi reiterated, "Remember, when one has doubts and is ready to give up, others must hold on and not give up. Only then will it last."

Rashi drove off, leaving Adi speechless with a lot to think about.

Marie and Natalie were at the local supermarket when they met Conrad Watson. It was a pleasant surprise for Marie after so many years. They started talking to Conrad. Natalie also felt happy seeing Conrad, but she kept mostly silent.

"I am a physician, now practicing in Berlin."

"Yes. I am aware of that. Natalie is also in Berlin."

"I know, she is now a big TV star, DE Media and all. I watch her shows sometimes."

The conversation continued for a few more minutes before Marie invited Conrad for evening tea at her home. Natalie didn't like that Marie invited Conrad; however, to her own surprise, she felt happy when Conrad accepted it.

On their drive back home, Marie was visibly happy and went on and on about how good Conrad was and that he had made a great career in Berlin, where Natalie stayed as well. Unlike Marie, Natalie was awfully quiet. She was intrigued as to why she felt such happiness upon meeting Conrad. Meeting Conrad had brought her respite from the harsh reality of a brewing break up with Adi. Natalie did not like it. She felt guilty for feeling that way.

Natalie and Conrad were high school sweethearts. They have been in the same school since childhood. Natalie was a year behind Conrad. They spent their schooling years without meeting or talking to each other until they reached high school.

In high school on the brink of adulthood, when the curiosity toward the opposite sex started growing, Conrad noticed her and got interested in this beautiful girl from the junior class. After that, Conrad expressed his liking for Natalie. As a teenager, it was a new and exciting experience for Natalie as well. She also ventured into her first romantic journey with Conrad. It lasted for a good two years of high school.

During these two years, Conrad was introduced to Marie and Bernhard. Marie liked Conrad and became fond of him. Conrad used to visit them to meet Natalie often, and Marie always welcomed him, while the protective father, Bernhard, inherently did not like Conrad much.

All was going well between them. However, a misunderstanding caused by a mutual friend led Natalie to believe that Conrad behaved below her principled expectations toward a girl, which strained their relationship. This, combined with the immaturity of young adults and their egos, led to an escalation of misunderstandings, eventually resulting in the breakup. The breakup was hurtful and difficult for both. Specifically, it was more hurtful for Natalie as her ideal belief and dream of a 'happily ever after' romantic story with Conrad fell short of her expectations. It was also hard on Marie because her dream for Natalie and Conrad was shattered.

After several years, with Natalie's breakup with Adi and Conrad Watson in town, Marie's hopes began to rekindle.

She had invited Conrad for coffee, hoping for Natalie and Conrad's spark to reignite.

Conrad visited Marie for tea. After some casual conversation, Marie made an excuse to leave Conrad and Natalie alone. Bernhard was at work. Conrad and Natalie took a while to warm up, as it was several years since they last met. It did not take long for them to get comfortable with one another once again. Natalie and Conrad had a long conversation about general topics and what they had been up to for the past several years. They fondly talked about their time together as well. After that, Natalie couldn't stop herself and poured her heart out before Conrad.

Natalie and Conrad kept meeting after this, both at Marie's home and outside.

I'll Win Her Back

"Amma, I am leaving tonight."

"You still have five more days."

"I need to go; something urgent has come up."

Adi had a sleepless night after meeting Rashi, but by dawn, he had made up his mind.

Harpreet tried to convince Adi to stay back and go to Germany as planned. Revathi was aware of what was going on in Adi's mind and did not try to convince him otherwise. In the evening, as Adi bent down to take Revathi's blessings, old memories of the time when Adi had left for Europe the last time clouded Revathi's mind. This time it was better as Adi wasn't upset at his parents while leaving. Adi was feeling slightly nervous but happy as he was going to win back Natalie.

Throughout his flight, Adi kept thinking about what he would say to Natalie when he met her. He kept thinking about how it would go with Natalie, which made him nervous. However, he was optimistic and never thought of an adverse outcome.

Upon landing in Berlin, Adi dropped his bag at his apartment and then rushed straight to Natalie's office. Natalie was not there. Upon inquiring, he found that Natalie had taken a week off to visit her mother. Adi took the first train out of

Berlin Central to visit Natalie. As Adi was traveling on the train, the memory of his last train travel on the same route with Natalie made him smile and filled his heart with love for Natalie. It was the train ride when he realized that he wanted to spend the rest of his life with her.

Adi immediately took a taxi to Marie and Bernhard's home as the train reached the destination.

As a taxi pulled over at Marie and Bernhard's home, he saw a young gentleman and Natalie coming out of the house's front door. He saw the gentleman lean forward and hug Natalie. It was a hug that lasted longer than normal. Then he kissed her on the cheek before leaving. It was Dr. Conrad Watson.

Adi's face was long and sad as he sat at the bar at Mizo's. Sameer sat next to him. The beer was flowing.

"It's over, Sameer, it's over."

"But I thought it was over earlier. You said so yourself when Natalie found out about Taiji."

"No, it's really over now."

"But last time before you went to India…"

"It doesn't matter what happened earlier. It's over now," Adi interrupted Sameer, irritated at his comments.

Sameer was still trying to wrap his head around what had happened when he suddenly realized.

"Hold on, when did you come back from India?"

"Today."

"But you were going to be here after 5 days."

"I wish I had returned as planned instead of rushing back to Berlin like a fool."

"Not sure about that comment," Sameer asked.

"I still feel you guys will fix things and be together. You are meant to be together. What makes you think it's over this time?"

"Because she is getting married."

"Getting married. What! To whom?"

"Does it matter?"

"Yes. It matters if the one she is marrying is not you."

"Of course, it's not me; it's some doctor named Watson."

"Dr. Watson, as in Sherlock Holmes. That's funny."

"Yes. Dr. Watson, as in Sherlock Holmes. Let's drop the topic, Sameer. OK. She has moved on. I should move on as well." Adi was annoyed and retorted back in anger.

Adi concluded the evening by getting up and leaving. He decided to walk back home. Sameer paid the bill and rushed out, worried about Adi.

"Sameer, I am fine. I think I will just walk back home. It's late. Malini must be waiting," Adi insisted, but Sameer could not leave his friend in this state. He went along with Adi.

Adi was sad and devastated. As he walked back listlessly toward his apartment, he was swinging between multiple emotions. At one instant, he regretted not reaching out to Natalie sooner and allowed her to slip away. At another moment, he felt angry at Natalie for not waiting long enough.

"If she really loved me, she could have waited. Why couldn't she reach out to me if I was acting stupid and not reaching out to her?"

Sameer ensured Adi reached his home safely before leaving. On his way back, he called Malini to inform her what had happened.

In the evening Adi missed three calls from Revathi. He was aware that Revathi must be eagerly waiting to hear what had transpired from his hurried rush back to Berlin. Adi intentionally did not received those calls because he did not want to talk about what had happened. Knowing well that his mother would be worried about him, he dropped a message saying, *All is well. It's late. We will talk tomorrow.* Revathi was awake and worried. She saw the message and replied, *Okay.*The next morning, Adi called Revathi. She was already at the university and about to enter her class.

Seeing Adi's call, she decided to skip the class and talk to Adi. She messaged Surabhi, her PhD student, to attend the graduate-level class instead.

Adi tried to put on a brave face while talking to Revathi, but his voice gave away his sadness. Adi concisely narrated what had happened with Natalie.

"Yes, I know," Revathi immediately regretted saying that.

"Of course you do," Adi retaliated with irritation.

Malini had informed Revathi about the events late last night.

"She is making a mistake. She loves you. Didn't you try to convince her?"

"Let it go, Amma. It's over. I did everything I could. But it's over," Revathi said. She realized how much Adi was hurting and wished she could help him in some way.

Agantuk

Sameer knew Adi well and realized that Adi needed his space now. He would not be ready to talk to anyone until he healed himself. Revathi also realized this; however, as a mother, she was worried and wanted someone to be with him. They had not talked since the call when he informed Revathi about Natalie getting married. There were a few casual messages from Revathi to which Adi had responded concisely in a few words. Adi was staying aloof. Revathi could feel that he was hurting, and it made her sad. She had also asked Malini and Sameer to take care of him.

Malini had invited Adi for dinner, which he had declined. Typically, Malini would get mad at Sameer's Mizo outing with Adi. However, this time Malini asked Sameer to take Adi to Mizo's. Adi declined that invitation as well.

Sameer had to bear the brunt of it from Malini.

"What kind of friend are you if you can't even convince him to have a drink or help your friend who is in so much trouble?"

It had been four weeks since the tragic day when he returned to Berlin from India. Adi made another call to Revathi. After exchanging greetings, Adi came straight to the point.

"Mum, I want to tell you something," Adi's voice was serious and flat.

"Yes, dear. Tell me," Revathi sounded concerned.

Receiving a call from Adi made Revathi happy. She felt it was a change in a positive direction.

"Amma, I am getting married."

"What? That sounds great. I am happy you and Natalie worked out things between you," Revathi was excited. However, she was a little confused as Adi sounded hesitant while telling this.

"Amma, it's not Natalie. I am marrying someone else," Revathi realized why he sounded hesitant.

"What? Who is she?" Revathi went from pleasant excitement to shock in moments.

"She works in my office," Revathi was surprised and shocked. She never thought Adi would do something as stupid as this. Deciding to marry someone as a rebound from his breakup with Natalie was stupid. Revathi believed that if he was trying to get back to Natalie by getting married since she was getting married, it was stupid. If Natalie had moved on, she would hardly care what Adi did. Revathi felt the urge to talk some sense into her stupid son, but she refrained from doing it right away as Adi would not listen to her. Instead, Revathi tried to know more about the girl. "I am getting late, Amma. I need to go now; we will talk about this later."

The information flow was reversed this time. Revathi called Malini immediately to inform her and inquire if she knew anything about it. She did not. Malini used to make Sameer tell her everything, especially on this matter, so she could confidently say Sameer knew nothing about it. Malini was shocked as well and felt Adi was making a big mistake.

I will talk to Sameer and see what we can do about this.

Over the years, Malini had developed a brotherly bond with Adi. She cared about Adi and Adi's well-being. All the effort that Malini had put into Adi's relationship was to see Adi happy and succeed in his love. It was out of care for Adi. Adi also admired Malini and felt she was the best thing that could have happened to his goofy friend Sameer.

Malini always wished Adi would come to her for advice in matters of his relationship rather than going to Sameer. She had no faith in Sameer's ability to advise in such matters. Of course, Adi felt more comfortable talking to his friend about this than to her. Sameer's failure to convince Adi not to marry Agantuk required her to take some drastic steps.

"Sameer, you are taking care of the kids today. And please call Adi and tell him I want to meet him today at Mizo's at 7."

Malini reached Mizo's little after 7. Adi was already seated. He had taken a table instead of sitting at the bar as Malini was coming.

"It feels so good to come out without kids. If you had not created such a mess, believe me, I would have partied today." Adi smiled. Malini got down to business right away without wasting any time.

"Why are you doing this, Adi? Why are you getting married in such a hurry?"

"I fell in love with her, and we thought, why delay? So, getting married."

"You are lying," Adi laughed at Malini's comment.

"Believe me, I am not. I am happy, and I am marrying someone whom I love dearly."

"Then why are you hiding her from us, from your mother? Let us meet her." Adi laughed again.

"No. Not happening. For a long time, everyone has been involved in my love stories. This time I am going to do it my way."

"Come on, Adi, don't do this. Imagine how worried and curious Taiji would be."

"Stop emotional blackmail, Malini. I am not telling anyone, and no one needs to be worried about me."

"But you are marrying someone you don't love in such a hurry as a rebound."

"You can think that, Malini, if you wish. I am in love with her, and I am marrying her."

"At least tell us who this girl is."

"No, no, no, I am not telling anything," Adi said. Adi had a certain childlike excitement about his secret. It did not appear just four weeks back; he was heartbroken and devastated. Adi seemed genuinely happy.

"So you are going to go round and round about this. You are neither going to change your mind about marrying her nor going to tell us more about her."

"Nope."

"Okay, then. No point in talking about it more. I am going to make the best out of my evening out without kids, and party." Malini emptied her beer glass and ordered a pitcher.

"You know I should do this more often. Go out with my friends for an evening out." Several pitchers, lots of conversation about random stuff, and lots of dancing on the dance floor later, she called it a night. It was late. Adi accompanied Malini and ensured she reached home safely.

A few days later, Adi called Revathi again. As usual, it was a video call. Revathi could not resist herself but talk about how she felt about his decision.

"Adi, I feel you should think one more time before jumping into this marriage. It is a big decision, and you cannot rush into it because of a breakup."

"Amma, it is too late for all that. I have made up my mind. In fact, I called to tell you that we are getting married on the 23rd."

"23rd of this month? That is three weeks from now!" Revathi reacted with an alarmed expression.

"Please tell Appa and start preparations to be here for the wedding."

Revathi was in shock. To her surprise, Adi sounded happy and appeared happy as well on the video call. She was intrigued, as the recent events and Adi's demeanor did not match. A month ago, he was devastated, and now he appeared so happy. He did not appear bitter at all. It did not look like a rebound marriage to despise Natalie. He appeared actually happy. It wasn't a facade. Revathi was glad to see Adi happy. However, she felt something did not add up in the equation.

"That's too soon, son."

"Yes, we wanted to get married as soon as we could. Do not worry about the preparations; we will manage everything here. You just be here."

"Adi, please tell us about who this girl is. Let us have a video call this evening. Invite her."

"No, Amma. You can meet her at the wedding when you are here." Adi did not want anyone to influence this one.

"At least you could tell us something about her," Revathi insisted. Adi thought for a moment and then replied.

"Her name is Agantuk, Agantuk Sharma. She works in our office. She is very pretty and well-mannered."

Revathi tried to inquire more, but Adi wasn't ready to give away anything else.

Harpreet was eager to talk about what conversation Revathi and Adi had earlier. He had only received a concise message from Revathi earlier, saying, "Adi called. He is getting married on the 23rd. We have to go. More when I get back. I'm going for a lecture now."

As usual, Harpreet was preparing coffee when Revathi reached home. Harpreet was eager to know the details, and Revathi was also eager to talk about it. She narrated everything about Adi's call, as soon as she came home.

"Do you think he is really happy?"

"He sounded and appeared happy."

"I wonder who this Agantuk girl is. And what kind of name is this Agantuk? It sounds Malaysian or Thai. Something like Tuktuk that we traveled in during our visit," Revathi laughed.

"It sounds like Indian Harpreet. It means visitor. Someone who visits for a purpose. What a thoughtful name."

"Oh, okay. Actually a nice name. But we do not know the purpose of her visit in Adi's life. We do not know who this girl is. Who her family is. I hope Adi knows what he is doing. It's a big decision. It worries me a bit," Harpreet paused, took a sip of coffee, and continued. "Either our son has really fallen in love within days of breaking up with Natalie, or he has become a very good actor."

"It's not that, Harpreet. I would know it in an instant if he was faking it. He looked really happy."

"Or he had got really good at faking emotions on your calls." Revathi gave a stern look to Harpreet.

"Well, in any case, there's nothing for us to do but pack our bags and join him in his happiness. Kids these days do not give you a choice. As parents, what we can do is show up when they invite." Aside from being worried for Adi, Harpreet was also not happy about how they were invited to their son's wedding, almost like guests.

Revathi did not react. She continued staring at her cup of coffee, lost in her thoughts, trying to make sense of what was happening.

"Probably this is a first; as parents, we are intrigued seeing our son happy and wondering how come he is happy. Emotions that kids put you through, I tell you, it's tough to be parents," Revathi got out of her thoughtful pause and smiled.

Since Adi was so elusive about the details of the girl he was planning to marry, Malini decided to take matters into her own hands. She decided to find out more about Agantuk, the name she came to know from Revathi. Malini and Sameer were at Adi's office. Malini forced Sameer to join her in the investigation against his will.

A young fashionable girl confidently walked out of the office elevator in the office lobby. She was tall and slim. She was sporting a pair of well-fitted dark-wash blue jeans. She paired them with a stylish, tucked-in white blouse with cute woven strings tied at her chest and hanging in the front. She was wearing chic ankle boots. Her white metal danglers were the only jewelry she wore. Her hair was tied in a smart bun, giving her a corporate look in an otherwise casual look.

The lady at the reception pointed toward the far end of the large corporate lobby.

"She is Agantuk."

Agantuk got out of the elevator and stopped to talk to someone as Sameer and Malini moved closer toward him.

"My God. She is pretty." Sameer stared at her with his mouth open. Malini gave a stern look, closing his mouth with her hand.

"Focus, Sameer. There is a problem. Don't you see it?"

"What? She looks fine. I don't see an issue if Adi is marrying a girl as pretty as her. He got lucky."

Malini got frustrated and exhaled through her mouth to maintain her composure instead of losing her temper toward Sameer.

"Be quiet and listen," Malini said, putting her finger on Sameer's mouth.

"She is too young. She must be barely 21 or 22. Probably fresh out of college."

Malini wanted to go and talk to Agantuk, but Sameer stopped her. Before they could settle the rift, Agantuk got out of the office building and disappeared into the crowd outside. The opportunity was lost.

Malini did meet Agantuk eventually without Sameer's knowledge. Everything from her meeting with Agantuk was reported back to Revathi.

Back to Berlin

Before they traveled abroad for their son's wedding, Harpreet and Revathi got busy preparing for the wedding and the travel. Revathi took care of packing, and Harpreet made the travel arrangements. Revathi packed their bags, which included thoughtfully selected special gifts for the bride and the groom. Adi had given very short notice, so they had to do everything in a hurry. Revathi had never dreamed about how Adi's wedding would be, but Harpreet felt they would have a big Punjabi wedding with a touch of Tamil Nadu traditions in it. The feeling got stronger recently after attending his nephew's Punjabi wedding in Chandigarh. But what was happening was totally unanticipated. They never thought they would be visiting Adi's wedding almost as guests going to the relatives' wedding. Harpreet regretted this more than Revathi. His mind was also consumed with doubts.

"Who was this woman their son had chosen to spend the rest of his life with?" The lack of familiarity worried Harpreet, casting a shadow over what should have been a moment of pure happiness. On the other hand, Revathi exuded a sense of calmness and serenity that felt almost annoying to Harpreet. Revathi was cheerful all through the preparation and tried to keep Harpreet positive and accepting of what was happening. At times, Harpreet would feel surprised at Revathi's calmness.

"Are you not feeling worried or even a bit anxious about this wedding and who the bride is?" Revathi would just smile and say, "Relax, everything will be all right. I am sure. I trust our son." Harpreet would shake his head sideways in disbelief every time he heard this from Revathi.

"Congratulations, Sir."

"Mr. Ironman. Thank you."

The news of Adi's upcoming marriage was spreading. Revathi had told Mala about their upcoming trip, and Mala told it to Baban. Baban was summoned urgently to take the clothes for ironing and return the next day on time for the trip.

"Sir Ji, you should have planned a wedding with pomp and pageantry in India. It is no fun there."

"I wish we had a big, fat Punjabi wedding for Adi. It is something worth attending."

"Yes, Sir".

"You should attend one. It is so much fun."

Revathi heard the conversation and commented, looking at Mala.

"I tell you, Mala, since he has attended his nephew's wedding in Chandigarh, all he can think of is a Punjabi wedding. Believe me, given a choice he would marry again to attend a Punjabi wedding."

Mala laughed.

"Yes, why not. We can get married again, Punjabi style. Anyways, the first time we got married was a boring wedding." Everyone laughed.

"Yes. Then Mala and I will also get to attend a Punjabi wedding," everyone laughed.

"Yes. Done deal. Anyway, with our son, there is nothing like that happening." Revathi could sense resentment, but she ignored it.

Finally, the day of travel arrived, and Harpreet and Revathi embarked on a journey filled with excitement and a touch of anxiety as they traveled abroad to attend their son's wedding. While the prospect of celebrating such a joyous occasion filled them with anticipation, there was a lingering sense of apprehension, particularly for Harpreet, who couldn't shake off the uncertainty of not knowing the bride-to-be.

"Relax, everything will be all right. I am sure. Trust me."

Harpreet and Revathi reached Berlin a day before the wedding. Adi was at Berlin airport to receive his parents.

There was almost complete silence in the cab for the full ride from the airport to Adi's house. Adi occasionally pointed at a monument or a building, explaining what it was to Harpreet. It was Harpreet's first trip to Berlin. With the elephant in the room not addressed, he was not interested in what Adi showed him. But Harpreet kept quiet as it was no use pestering Adi now, just a day ahead of the wedding when he had not told them details about Agantuk until then. Adi knew why Harpreet was quiet and upset. However, he did not venture into the topic as well.

"Harpreet Ji, enjoy the views. It's a wonderful city," Revathi tried to cheer Harpreet.

Adi was surprised at how well Revathi took his sudden venture into marriage. He expected some anxiousness and disapproval regarding his wedding from Revathi. The lack of disapproval, though in his favor, almost made Adi unhappy.

Once Harpreet and Revathi were settled upon reaching home, Revathi asked about the plan for the next day.

"No change in the plan that we discussed for tomorrow. Right?"

"Yes. No change."

Earlier, Adi had discussed the wedding plan and involved his parents in the planning. He did not want them to get involved and talk to his future wife. But as a good son, he did not want to exclude them from planning the whole thing, which was the biggest occasion of his life and theirs too.

"We will go to the courthouse for the wedding at 10 a.m., and then head for lunch at the India Club, one of the best fine-dining places for authentic Indian food in Berlin.

Harpreet assumed the place was chosen because Agantuk is also Indian.

"Bridegroom, his parents, bride, bride's parents, her best friend, Sameer, Malini, and kids, only these people will be there," Revathi confirmed. Adi was surprised that Revathi mentioned the bride's best friend. He was sure that he had never mentioned a friend to Revathi. But he did not delve too deeply into that matter.

At the Schmidt household, things were relaxed due to the lack of a formal church wedding followed by a reception dinner. Marie wasn't happy about it. She wanted a formal Christian wedding. Natalie and Conrad both had decided otherwise. Instead, they had planned to get married in the courthouse, in the presence of only the immediate family. Natalie and Conrad did not even agree to an elaborate reception. The post-wedding reception was also limited to lunch with the immediate family. Marie had sought intervention from Conrad's parents on the matter, but her phone calls to Conrad's mother were unanswered. Conrad explained to Marie that his parents were traveling to East Asia and would return only a day before the wedding. Marie found it weird, but Natalie gave a stern stare to Marie, suggesting her into silence and not making a fuss about it. Marie had unwillingly obliged.

Since the day Marie was informed about Natalie and Conrad getting married, she wanted to talk to Conrad's parents. Conrad was very elusive about it. Upon insisting on several occasions, Conrad gave in and arranged a call between his mother and Marie.

Earlier, Natalie and Conrad had visited Marie and Bernhard in Berlin to inform them that they had decided to get married. Marie was very happy to hear it, but Bernhard was skeptical. He knew they were high school sweethearts, but he also remembered how heartbroken Natalie had been just weeks before. Bernhard said nothing. Natalie sensed the worry Bernhard was feeling for her. Later that evening, when Bernhard was alone in his study, Natalie went to meet him. It was the same study where Bernhard had had a serious talk with Adi when Natalie had first introduced him.

She went and sat at the study table next to Bernhard. He was sitting on a chair at the study table.

"So, my little girl is getting married."

"Not so little, Dad," Natalie replied while fidgeting with a pen she took from the desk.

"Yes, not so little anymore," Bernhard was emotional. He stared at Natalie in the eyes with a worried look and spoke.

"I don't want you to make any compromises, darling. I want you to be happy for the rest of your life."

Natalie looked back into Bernhard's eyes and replied, "I will be, Dad."

The reply and the confident look in Natalie's eyes were reassuring for Bernhard. It was an emotional moment between father and daughter.

"Why don't you come and stay with us for a few days before the wedding?" Bernhard asked her to change the mood in the room.

Natalie visited Bernhard and Marie for a few days before the wedding. She wanted to live with her parents for a few days before the wedding. Caroline, Natalie's best friend, had accompanied her.

Marie wished that Natalie wore her wedding dress for the wedding. Natalie did not mind it, even at a courthouse, to make her mother happy. After all, nothing else was happening as per Marie's wishes. The tailor was visited, and the dress was altered to fit Natalie. Matching footwear was purchased. That was the only preparation needed for the wedding. The rings were already purchased in Berlin.

They all left for Berlin a day before the wedding.

The Wedding

Adi and the group sat in the third row from the end. Adi sat in the middle with Sameer to his left and Revathi to his right. Harpreet and Malini sat next to their soulmates, respectively, in the same row.

"Look, who's sitting there," Sameer whispered to Adi.

"Who? Where?"

"There. It's Natalie."

"I know."

"What do you mean? I know. What's going on?"

By this time, everyone in the group had noticed Natalie sitting across the hall five rows ahead of them. She was sitting with her parents, Marie and Bernhard, and Caroline.

"Yes, Adi, what do you mean you know? What's going on?" Malini bent across Sameer and repeated as Harpreet and Revathi stared at Adi. Malini tried to appear worried and confused as if she had no knowledge of what was happening.

"Calm down everyone. I knew she was going to get married today. But don't worry, I will get married before her. She couldn't even wait a few days for me before agreeing to marry someone. I will show her who gets married first. Who needs her," Adi tried to appear serious and angry.

Concerned for Adi, Sameer again tried to explain to Adi about the mistake he was making by getting married in vengeance.

"Adi, you are getting married for the wrong reasons. You…"

"Sameer, stop. It's too late. No use now."

Malini was still leaning forward across Sameer, listening to what Adi said.

Harpreet was bent over Revathi to hear the conversation. He whispered, "Yes. It's stupid," with a frustrated and concerned look on his face.

"Everyone, calm down. Let it happen, what's happening," Revathi concluded.

"Thank you, Amma."

This ended the momentary commotion within the group, and there was silence again, each thinking and trying to wrap their head around what was happening from their perspective.

The bride and groom's names were occasionally announced as they were called for their appointment at the registrar's office in the courthouse.

A few minutes passed. There was still no sign of Agantuk, her parents, and her best friend. Harpreet got worried.

"Aren't Agantuk and her parents late? Do we have time?"

"I got a message from her. They are on their way. They will be here in 15 minutes. We have time."

Again, there was silence as they were lost in their thoughts, each one intermittently stealing a glance at Natalie and her family as they waited.

A few minutes later, Sameer noticed Natalie's father turning around and looking for something.

Sameer whispered, "It appears Natalie's husband and family are also late."

"Mind your own business. We have nothing to do with it now," Malini curtly interrupted Sameer before the conversation continued.

Bernhard turned around again. This time his eyes locked with Adi. He quickly looked away and whispered something to Natalie and her mother. Everyone in Adi's group noticed this. Moments later, Natalie, Caroline, and her mother turned around despite Bernhard's warning not to turn around and look all at once. Everyone in one group had eye contact with concerned people in the other group. Each one gave a mixed expression with a nervous smile.

Sameer whispered in a prolonged singing sort of way, "Awkward."

Both the groups settled back in silence after the awkward encounter of stares. A few minutes later, a young, handsome gentleman walked in and greeted Natalie's group. He was well dressed in a smart black suit. Bernhard got up, and they exchanged pleasantries while shaking hands. He then bent down to hug Natalie and greeted everyone else.

"Look, Sherlock's assistant has come," Sameer remarked.

Malini hushed her husband.

It was evident to everyone that this must be Natalie's future husband. Though it was not clear to them why he was alone.

The group sat there quietly, observing what was happening. They saw Conrad explaining something to Natalie's parents which they could not understand. Revathi noticed Caroline staring at Conrad with a sparkle in her eyes, revealing to Revathi that Caroline liked what she was seeing and was attracted to Conrad. As the group settled, Conrad sat next to Caroline, and both started chatting. The group felt that was weird.

"Another love story brewing," she thought and smiled to herself.

It was just 15 minutes since they had all settled at the registrar's office, but with the awkwardness of the situation and so many thoughts running through each of their minds, it felt like an hour to everyone.

Harpreet felt particularly anxious upon seeing Natalie's to-be husband, Conrad.

"Agantuk and her parents are nowhere to be seen," Harpreet muttered in frustration.

"Relax. Everything will be fine," Revathi repeated the sentence that Harpreet had been hearing for the past couple of weeks. She had the same carefree, peaceful smile on her face.

That annoyed Harpreet to the core. But before he could vent his frustration, he heard a soft voice.

"Hello everyone. Sorry, I got a bit late. I hope they did not announce our names yet."

Everyone turned around.

Agantuk stood there with a beaming smile in a traditional pink Kanjivaram silk saree with an embroidered, fashionably crafted, slightly revealing blouse. Sameer stared at her with his mouth open. Malini gave a stern look, closing his mouth with her hand.

Revathi and Harpreet were pleasantly surprised and impressed to see Agantuk in traditional Indian attire.

But Adi seemed unhappy about it.

"Why in a saree? We discussed something else."

Agantuk leaned her head slightly, shrugged her shoulders, and gave a sorry expression on her face.

Everyone else ignored Adi's comment.

It was Natalie's group's turn now to see what was happening. Everyone turned around to see Adi's bride.

Agantuk bent with a namaste to seek Revathi and Harpreet's blessings.

"No, no. Don't touch our feet," Revathi reacted.

"God bless you, dear. You look beautiful," Harpreet was impressed by her looks but had his doubts.

"Where are your parents?"

"They will be here shortly."

Sameer vacated the seat and sat on the other side of Malini so that Agantuk could sit next to Adi. Revathi suggested letting Agantuk sit next to her. She sat between Revathi and Adi, her arm linked with Adi's. The two ladies started chatting.

Bernhard, Marie, and Caroline turned their heads to take a look at Agantuk. Natalie and Conrad did not turn around to see what was happening. Probably, Natalie was hurting to see Adi with someone else, and Conrad was not interested in Natalie's ex-boyfriend.

A while later, as Agantuk leaned to the other side to talk to Adi, Harpreet whispered to Revathi, "What kind of family is this? They did not come together. Her parents are late and let her come alone."

To Harpreet's annoyance, Revathi only said, "Relax. Everything will be fine."

As both groups waited impatiently for their names to be called, the clerk came into the waiting hall and called for the next couple.

"Aditya Sodhi and Natalie Schmidt"

The group on both sides stared at Adi and Natalie in disbelief. Adi and Natalie had big smiles on their faces as they got up, heeding the clerk's call for the next couple to be married.

"This is our way of saying thank you. Thank you for all the meddling in our romcom. The meddling that we did not need in bringing us together," Adi whispered sarcastically, looking at Revathi. Revathi silently smiled back.

Adi and Natalie were married in the next 15 minutes.

The Wedding Gift

At night in their room, Natalie and Adi were reminiscing on their journey from the first time they met at a café in Berlin to the wedding. Natalie was feeling excited. The feeling of being married to Adi was still sinking in.

"Let's unwrap the gifts."

Adi protested unsuccessfully.

Earlier in the day, after the wedding, the group went to the India Club restaurant for lunch, and then everyone returned to Adi's house for coffee. Everyone showered the newlywed couple with gifts. The air was filled with joy and laughter as they all gathered to celebrate the newlyweds. Everyone shared their stories of Adi and Natalie's journey and their involvement in bringing this journey to fruition. Not everything was shared.

As the sun set, everyone left, leaving the young couple alone. Revathi and Harpreet had planned to stay at Sameer's place to give them privacy.

Natalie and Adi opened the gift boxes. The gifts included household items, personalized gifts, and cash.

One of the boxes was from Revathi. Natalie eagerly opened the wrapped gift box. The indigo-blue jewelry box was inside with the familiar Swarovski swan inscribed on top. Inside the box was a pair of earrings.

"Wow, this is beautiful," Adi exclaimed, looking at the earrings. Unlike Natalie, Adi did not have a keen eye for jewelry. Natalie was shocked.

"How could this be? How is this possible?" Natalie exclaimed. Adi was confused.

Underneath the earring, there was a note. Natalie read aloud.

Dearest Natalie,

Here is something to match the Swarovski pendant that Adi gifted you. My love and support for you will always match Adi's, if not surpass it.

Wish you a married life full of love and passion.

Love,
Dr. Revathi (Amma)

Adi and Natalie stared at the note in disbelief. The box contained Swarovski earrings, the design of which matched the pendant that Adi had gifted her.

"How did she know it was me that you were getting married to? We told no one. Not even Sameer."

She paused and then thoughtfully said, "We have been outsmarted by Dr. Revathi, dear."

Upon realizing that their scheme to deceive everyone had completely failed, Adi and Natalie could not help but burst into laughter.

Adi was still puzzled and could not let go. Adi immediately took his phone and messaged Revathi.

"How?"

Revathi was expecting the message from Adi. She promptly replied.

Dear Adi,

"Don't trouble yourself with 'HOW'. Consider your marriage to Natalie as a blessing from three goddesses: Goddess Rashi, Goddess Malini, and Goddess Revathi :)."

I wish both of you a happy married life full of love and passion. Good night."

Love,
Amma.

Adi read the message and smiled to himself. All the events since his big fight with Natalie flashed in his mind.

The Scheming Unfolds

Adi was in Mumbai after heartbreak, with a promise from Revathi that they would not discuss the matter. Revathi knew how much Adi was hurting inside, even though Adi put on a bold face. Revathi could not see her son suffer. She understood that his ego was preventing him from trying to mend things with Natalie. She had to act.

It was not difficult for Revathi to find Rashi's phone number through Adi and Rashi's mutual friend, who was still in touch with Adi. Revathi met Rashi and told her about Adi's love story and the difficult situation the couple had put themselves in. Rashi had found love in her husband after separation from Adi. She wished that Adi would also find love and happiness. Rashi was eager to help.

"You see how stupid both of them are acting. They are throwing away such a wonderful relationship. It is so immature."

"True. I wish I could help."

"As a matter of fact, you can."

Rashi meeting Adi at the Eastend Mall was not a coincidence. Meeting Rashi changed his mind, and it made Adi rush back to Germany to mend things with Natalie.

As his taxi pulled over at Marie and Bernhard's home, Adi saw a young gentleman and Natalie coming out of the house. He saw the gentleman lean forward and hug Natalie—a hug that lasted longer than normal. Then he kissed her on the cheek before leaving. Adi could not recognize who it was in the dimly lit driveway of the house. It was Dr. Conrad Watson.

Adi waited in the taxi for a while longer, fighting the urge to return after what he saw. The taxi driver interrupted his train of thought. Adi paid the driver, walked to the house, and knocked on the door. Marie opened the door. She gave Adi a stern look, knowing that he had hurt Natalie. Marie did not know the reason for the breakup.

"Natalie, Adi is here."

Natalie was instantly elated before the reality of her fight with Adi sank back in the next moment.

"What do you want?"

"Can we talk?"

After separating from Adi, the past few weeks were very painful for Natalie. She also wanted to talk and mend ways with Adi. Marie was standing there witnessing what was happening.

"Let's go out for a walk."

It was dark outside. Winter had brought in early darkness. It was only 5 p.m. As Natalie and Adi strolled out in the dim light, the memory of his strolls with Rashi flashed momentarily in Adi's mind.

"What's with the guy?" Adi asked, referring to Conrad.

"Is that what you've come to talk about?"

"No Sorry."

There was silence for a few seconds as they continued to walk.

"I am sorry, Natalie. I should have told you who my mother was. I missed it the first time, and then it was too late to tell. I am sorry. I love you."

Natalie burst into laughter considering the mess that got created and thinking about what Adi would have gone through when she went on and on about Dr. Revathi during that period and he could not tell her that she was his mother. Natalie realized that Adi did not hide it intentionally and got stuck in the mess unintentionally.

Adi, confused, stopped walking and turned toward Natalie, raising his hands and gesturing, "What?"

Natalie gave a peck on his lips and said, "I love you too."

It took Adi a few moments to realize it was time to forget what had happened and that they were back on. This brought a big smile to his face, which he reciprocated with a peck, too. "I love you."

"But I want to warn you. No more hiding things from me. Else there won't be any second chances."

"Never."

They continued walking, holding hands. Adi was content and in bliss, but Natalie's mind was racing with a wicked idea.

"For a long time, our parents have been meddling with our lives. Your mum in all this that has happened. And mine, too, matchmaking and pestering me into getting married. I want to give it back to them."

"What do you mean?"

"Let's not tell them that we got together and pretend we are getting married to someone else?"

Over the next few days, Natalie and Adi worked out the details of their plan. The hurried marriage date was finalized. Revathi and Harpreet were invited. Conrad was brought in confidence. Marie and Bernhard were made to believe Natalie was getting married to Conrad, a German by blood and race. Revathi and Harpreet would want to know the bride. Agantuk, Adi's mentee and junior colleague in the office, was coached to play her part on the wedding day to give a dramatic high to the parents further before the truth was unraveled.

Adi was skeptical about the whole plan.

"I hope we are doing the right thing."

A fiery streak in Natalie had taken over. She was determined to go through with the plan.

"We are doing this. For all we have gone through," Natalie was determined.

"You think so?"

"Do not worry. All is well that ends well."

Earlier,

"You do know, Conrad, that I cannot marry you," Natalie told Conrad when Marie invited him to meet Natalie after her heartbreak and hoped they would get together.

"Neither can I," Conrad cleared the air.

They were high school sweethearts but drifted apart after their breakup. However, their friendship was rekindled after they met at the supermarket and spent some time together. Conrad had become Natalie's confidant as in their high school days. Conrad visited Marie's home often while he was in town. Natalie used to discuss Adi and how much she still loved him.

After Adi and Natalie patched up their differences, Conrad was read in on the devilish scheme to fool Adi and Natalie's parents. Being a good friend of Natalie, he agreed to pretend to marry Natalie and visit the courthouse on the wedding day, pretending to be Natalie's husband.

Marie was happy to have a German son-in-law.

Though Conrad had agreed to this small game with Natalie, he had no intention of involving his parents in this game. Neither did Natalie or Adi. However, they did understand that Marie's insistence on meeting Conrad's parents was a reasonable expectation. Marie had insisted on meeting Conrad's parents when Conrad and Natalie had announced their decision to get married. Since then Natalie and Conrad had returned back to Berlin. But Marie had continued to pester Conrad over the phone to arrange a call or meeting with his parents. Conrad was running out of excuses and was under tremendous pressure. Conrad insisted on meeting Natalie and Adi. They met at Mizo's.

"I cannot take it any longer. I am running out of excuses," visibly nervous Conrad complained.

Adi and Natalie realized they could not escape this without Marie suspecting something fishy.

"We will have to arrange for Conrad's mother."

"Who?"

"Beautiful lady who will pretend to be your bride."

"Agantuk. How's that possible?"

"Over the phone. You said once that her German is good."

"That works," Conrad's voice expressed excitement and relief.

"Anyway, I have made an excuse that they are traveling and could not meet in person," Conrad continued.

Agantuk was coached on the topics of conversation and given a cheat sheet on answers to specific questions. It was rehearsed and practiced multiple times before the actual call. Agantuk's number was shared with Marie. Adi, Natalie, and Conrad were present with Agantuk when the call happened to help her out in case Agantuk got stuck with something. The bottom line was to steer clear of any in-person meeting that Marie would suggest. Excuses were prepared and rehearsed.

Agantuk managed the call well.

Marie and Bernhard's cell phone number and home phone number were given to Agantuk to avoid unsupervised calls from Marie to Conrad's fake mother.

"No matter what, please do not answer any calls from these numbers."

"Hello Agantuk. I am Malini."

Malini and Agantuk were sitting at a café near Adi's office. It was the same café near Adi's office where Adi had met Natalie for the first time.

Earlier, Adi's sudden declaration of marriage had shocked everyone. His transition from heartbreak to a happy, to-be-wed boy was very sudden. Revathi was too good at face reading and understanding voice modulation to be fooled by an act. She realized through her video calls with Adi that his happiness was real. He was not faking it. Revathi knew her son too well to know that Adi would never decide to jump into a rebound marriage. It always took Adi a while to open up and commit to anyone. Hence, Revathi was sure it was impossible for Adi to go from heartbreak to committing to marry someone in three to four weeks. She knew something was fishy.

Revathi was curious to know what was really happening. She wanted to keep Harpreet out of this to avoid unnecessary explanations to him. She only had a name, Agantuk, from Adi to unravel the mystery. Malini, her confidant on the ground in Berlin, came to Revathi's rescue.

Malini wanted to go and talk to Agantuk during their first encounter, but Sameer stopped her. Before they could settle the rift, Agantuk got out of the office building and disappeared into the crowd outside. Malini was determined to meet her and get to the root of Adi and Agantuk's marriage. The following day Malini went to Adi's office and waited in the lobby. This time she decided not to take Sameer along. She did not trust him to keep his mouth shut in front of Adi. It was evening, and gradually, people were trickling out after their day's work. She carefully placed herself in the corner, covering her face with a book to ensure Adi did not see her waiting when he left the office.

After an hour-long wait, Agantuk arrived from the elevator. Before she could approach Agantuk, she saw her rush out of the building. She was wearing a leather jacket, washed jeans, and long boots. Agantuk went out of the building, hugged and kissed a boy waiting outside on a motorcycle. Then she put on a helmet, and both zoomed away on the motorcycle. Malini saw this through the building's glass façade.

"The plot thickens, my dear Watson," Malini whispered to herself as she saw the girl Adi said he was getting married to riding away with another man.

The following day, Malini waited again at Adi's office. This time she was alert not to miss Agantuk. As Agantuk got out of the elevator, she rushed to meet her.

"Hello Agantuk. I am Malini, Adi's sister-in-law."

"Hello, Malini," Agantuk was surprised and a little scared.

"Congratulations on your engagement to Adi."

"Thank you," Agantuk hesitated. She was getting uncomfortable. Malini could read it on her face.

"Let's go for a coffee."

"No, I am in a rush. I need to go."

"You'd better come with me, or else I will let your parents know about your engagement to Adi," Malini threatened Agantuk with a cold whisper in his ears.

She continued, "I am sure they do not know it. They will be so happy to know that their princess is getting married. Also, they will be glad to know you have a bike-riding prince charming on the side too." Agantuk almost turned white listening to Malini.

"Believe me, I am serious. If I can find you, I can find your parents as well." In reality, Malini could find Agantuk easily because Adi had told Revathi her name and that she worked in his office.

It was a wild chance that Malini took to make Agantuk talk. It hit the bull's-eye.

Scared, Agantuk agreed to go for a coffee with Malini. Over coffee, Agantuk disclosed that she was not getting married to Adi.

"Adi had only requested me to show up at the wedding in torn jeans and a crop top to shock his parents at the wedding." The thought of Malini telling her parents about her small role with Adi and her biker boyfriend made Agantuk very nervous. She nervously continued.

"He had assured me that I would not have to meet his family or talk to them on the phone to participate in his lie," Agantuk was almost in tears as she replied.

"Who is he getting married to? Is it Natalie?" Malini asked sternly.

"Yes."

Malini was elated listening, getting an affirmative answer to her question. By this time, Agantuk had already started crying. Malini felt pity for Agantuk. She consoled him.

"Don't worry. We are good. Relax," Malini tried to console Agantuk but in vain.

Revathi met Agantuk upon visiting Berlin for Adi's wedding and gave her a traditional pink Kanjivaram silk saree. Revathi befriended Agantuk during their short meeting. That was an art in which Revathi was second to none. To play with Adi and Natalie's plan to tease them, Revathi asked Agantuk to wear the saree to the court on the wedding day instead of torn jeans and a crop top. Agantuk was happy to play a reverse prank on Adi.

The Interwoven Stories

The Closed Window

The din of the kids filled the festive home with cheer and joy. But she was not part of the gang of kids today. She sat there alone in the loft, crying, and her father was uneasy and sad downstairs.

It was the festival of Pongal in the traditional household in the 1970s. The world and India had entered the modern era of the 1970s. It was a day of family gatherings, celebrations, and prayers. For children, the day was even more special. It was a day for them to get together and have fun at the old family home. A home that was an anchor that brought the large family together. The family had spread around the globe but each one of them still felt the old house was their home and it was the place where all of them met. The great-grandparents built it, the grandparents grew up there, and the parents after that. Some of the fourth-generation kids were now growing up in the house. Then there were cousins and their cousins in the age group of 5 to 16 from the widespread family tree that visited the house for the festivals. All put together, the total number of kids that gathered went into double digits.

A while ago, she was playing downstairs with her cousins. Her laughter was the loudest, towering over her cousin's voice echoing through the tall ceiling of the inner hall of the house. But now she was in tears and confined to the room in the loft. It was an old two-story independent house with wooden windows and walls painted with white lime. The large teak beams decorated the ceiling of the ground floor supporting the floor above. The house had a large inner hall with a tall ceiling two floors high. The inner hall had a large door opening into the garden at the backside. The garden was kind of a rough terrain with large old trees, shrubs, and flowering plants with Tulasi planted on a three-foot-tall structure in the middle. The loft had a large window overlooking the inner hall. The window had been closed for years now for the fear of kids leaning and falling over. Gradually, the window got hidden behind a cupboard, a table, and assorted things as the family grew and more space was needed. The clutter in front of the window would have to give way to that auspicious day like the years-old traditions that had cluttered the lives of the young twinkling lives.

A while ago, her father, the younger of the two brothers currently staying in the house, was busy doing chores in the house. Additionally, he had taken upon himself a bigger and tougher responsibility of keeping the children in the house in check. If left unchecked, they had the capacity to turn the day and occasion into chaos. He was the loving Vishu kaka for the children in the household. His elder brother, dressed in the traditional prayer attire, would perform the prayers. Vishu kaka had restricted the kids to the inner hall. The outdoor garden would have been the ideal place to let kids run loose to avoid any chaos inside the house, but the kids would get all dusty and sweaty if allowed to play outdoors. The tall ceiling of the hall allowed for good airflow and kept it cooler than the rest of the house. It was a big hall with a large old swing suspended from the tall ceiling in the middle of the hall. For the occasion, the swing was removed to free up the hall for lunch. Vishu had restricted children from running about in the rest of the house, especially the pooja room. Every so often, Vishu had to go and check in the inner hall and ask the children to make less noise.

A while ago, women in the house were chatting in the kitchen while preparing lunch for the festive occasion. Recipes were being discussed, and instructions were sought from elders in the house. A certain aunt fond of gossip had new stories to tell about a distant relative, neighbor, or acquaintance in general, which the women fondly savored. There was an occasional time check and tradition check given by the loving yet strict grandmother. Everything going on in the old house on the festive occasion was perfect until a clash of tradition and liberation happened. Vishu's elder daughter, Revathi, was in the common room in the loft, now crying, and Vishu was not happy about it. All the concerned people were going through different emotions. While the rest of the family members went on with the festivities, the grandmother was angry, the father was emotional, the daughter was sad, and the mother was indifferent to her daughter's emotional ordeal.

Just an hour ago, the cooking for the grand prasadam (sacred food offering to God) was progressing well, and so was the pooja. The roasting of the ghee, sugar, and sooji filled the house with the tempting smell of the prasad. Revathi's mom asked a certain gossip aunt to carry the prepared prasad to the pooja room and clear the kitchen platform for some other work. Just then, Revathi and her younger cousin came running into the kitchen to have some water. It was hot, and all the running and playing made the kids thirsty.

An aunt said, "Instead, tell Revathi to take the prasad; my hands are soiled with the mixing of the flour."

"No, let it be; I will take it," said Revathi's mum.

Revathi was almost 13, and the aunt thought she was old enough to help a little in the kitchen instead of running around the house playing and making mischief. She thought Revathi's mum was too protective of her daughter and not giving her any responsibilities. The rest of the women were listening to this conversation in the kitchen while the grandmother was instructing the kids not to drink water too quickly. Once Revathi was done having water, the aunt taunted.

"Revathi, you are old enough. Start helping your mother with some work in the kitchen. Please carry the prasad to the pooja room and give it to your uncle."

"It's not that; she is a good girl. She helps me all the time. But today she can't."

Listening to this hell broke loose in the festive household. Grandmother got very angry and started scolding her daughter-in-law for just allowing Revathi in the kitchen, let aside touching the prasad. She even started scolding Revathi for not understanding the customs and that she should not be playing with the cousins. Grandmother asked her to go upstairs to the loft and not play with her cousins or touch anything. Revathi was shocked at the sudden outburst of her grandmother and started crying. More than feeling scared, she felt embarrassed. It was all new to her, all the biological changes that her body was going through and then this sudden treatment of isolation by her grandmother was beyond her.

"Go to the loft and stay there all day. Do not touch anything or anyone. You will have your food upstairs today," ordered the grandmother.

She ran out of the kitchen and up the stairs to the loft. She ran past her father, who was coming to the kitchen to see what the noise was about. Vishu tried to stop her, but she did not.

Vishu went to the kitchen to check on what had happened. His mother was still very angry and gave an earful to her daughters and daughters-in-law, especially Revathi's mother. She said she would not tolerate such disregard of the customs. Listening to his mother's outburst, Vishu got the inkling of what had happened. It made Vishu very upset and sad. However, he did not speak up to his mother. For one, he did not want an argument on the festive day, but more so he and his siblings had never spoken up to their parents ever. That was how they were brought up. While Vishu and his brothers and sisters were growing up, elders were the important people in the family. His grandparents had the highest authority and respect. After his grandparents, his parents claimed that position. Kids did not have any say or position in the house, let alone being the most important people in the family that kids are in the modern days.

Vishu walked out of the kitchen and back to the pooja room. He was feeling very sad about what had happened. Revathi was his beloved daughter, and what she must be going through emotionally made him very sad and restless.

Revathi's mother was from the same generation as Vishu and was also raised in a household where elders were the most important people. That training carried on when she married and came to the Vishu household. She never spoke up to her mother-in-law. She kept quiet though she felt a little sad for her daughter's embarrassment. But she was more accepting of the customs and felt that is how things are for daughters. She experienced it herself when she was growing up and so should her daughters and all other girls. She took the prasad to the pooja room and went on with her work.

Revathi was still crying upstairs in the dimly lit loft. Little light came in through the small ventilation window close to the ceiling. The bigger window overlooking the downstairs hall was closed. She could hear her cousins playing in the hall downstairs through the closed window behind the stacked old furniture. She did not understand the custom nor did she care. She wanted to play with her cousins. But she could not. Vishu was getting restless downstairs. He wanted to go to the loft and hold his daughter. He wanted to console her. He wanted to explain to her and answer any questions that Revathi might have about the injustice that was done to her by her grandmother. He very well knew he would not have any valid answers to her questions, and he would have to make up some excuses in the name of customs and traditions. But Vishu could not go up and console her as he was helping and assisting his brother in the pooja, and hence hugging his daughter would not go well with his mother. Hell would break loose.

Kids were playing, pooja was going on, and elders were chatting on various topics. But Vishu's mind was engrossed in thinking about his daughter. Vishu was pacing downstairs in and out of the pooja room. Crossing the stairs, he could hear Revathi crying gently, gasping for breath as she continued to cry for a long time. Vishu's heart sank hearing his little princess cry and no one to console her. Vishu was an emotional person and in the last 13 years that Revathi was in his life, he could never bear seeing his daughter in pain.

He heard his daughter complain while crying, "I want to play with everyone."

Hearing this, Vishu could not stop himself. He climbed up the stairs to the hall. He saw Revathi lying on the bed hiding her face in her palms, crying and repeating "I just want to play." Vishu turned around, went to the clutter in front of the window, and started clearing the window. He pushed the cupboard to one side. It was heavy. It just moved an inch. He had misjudged the weight of the cupboard. He tried again with a little more strength. This time it moved a little more. Then he dug his feet hard on the floor and pushed with all his strength, making a big grunting noise as he pushed. The voice was heard downstairs by everyone, kids in the hall and elders in the pooja room alike. Women in the kitchen did not hear much of it. This time the cupboard moved a significant distance, and it was out of his way, clearing up the area in front of the window.

Vishu stepped to the window and started clearing up the spiderwebs from the window shutters with quick movements of his hands. It was as if trying to clear the web of tradition that had gripped the women for ages. He unlatched and opened the large window. The rectangular beam of light entered the room through the opened window, lighting up the dark room. The beam of light fell directly on the bed while Revathi was crying as if enlightening her life.

Kids downstairs cheered upon seeing Vishu in the upper window, oblivious to the emotions and drama that had unfolded in the past 30 minutes. Vishu did not react.

"This is the princess's window overlooking the palace ballroom," Vishu said in a muffled voice to Revathi and rushed downstairs to hide his teary eyes.

Minutes later, Revathi was upstairs at the window playing with her cousins downstairs in the hall.

The sound of her laughter brought a smile to Vishu's face and peace to his mind.

The experience subconsciously shaped Revathi's outlook toward the world and empowered her to shape her own life according to her wishes. Years later, she married Harpreet, ensuring that her family did not dictate the course of her life.

Little Dreams

Pedaling his cycle down the busy road bustling with cars from edge to edge, he did not care, hear, or feel the noise of the traffic or the pollution on his journey back from work. He was happy. He was busy all day and had earned a good remuneration for his work. Shivkumar was a daily wage laborer. He was not starving poor, but he was not well-off either. He made just enough to survive. His evening meal did not depend on what he earned and carried home each day. But there was no room for any luxury. He could afford to celebrate an occasion either by taking his family to a movie in a single-screen cinema theater, not an expensive multiplex, or having dinner at a roadside stall or sharing a cake with his family. Not all at the same time.

Shivkumar had an extraordinary day. He had earned a good amount from the day's work. He thought, with some earlier savings, maybe he could fulfill his son's long-time wish on his birthday the next day. A luxury that his son had dreamed of and mentioned several times since the day he first saw it on television, standing outside the glass window of an upscale consumer electronics store. Shivkumar had not seen his son craving for anything else so much and wondered what a 30-second advertisement on television did for his son to yearn for it even after so many days.

Whenever his son asked about his wish, Shivkumar only had stories to tell. At times Shivkumar would say the shop would be closed due to a national holiday that no one had heard about. Then, other times, Shivkumar would give an excuse that the chef would go on a holiday because his mother was sick, or the chef got hurt while cutting vegetables, or simply because he was too tired. Sometimes he pretended to come home very tired and ill and sleep early. He would leave home early to avoid the question or hope to get some opportunity to put in more sweat and get home something more than the daily necessities of survival. Anything extra that he earned, he added to the treasure he had started accumulating the day he realized his son's birthday wish was a real one and not a passing one that he would forget. Observing the glitz and glamour of the not-so-underprivileged, his son would wish for several things every day, and then these wishes would die and be replaced by new ones. But eating a large-size cheesy pizza along with coke was something that lingered in his mind for weeks, not days. It brought a sparkle to his eyes whenever he described the visuals he saw in the pizza advertisement on the television. It was not a passing desire. This one had stuck on.

As Shivakumar approached close to his house, he swirled his bicycle toward the left trying to avoid a car that had braked suddenly. His leg slightly brushed the tail of the car, but he maintained his balance and pedaled on. Nearby, two young boys in dirty, torn clothes were playing by the side of the road as he hurried back toward his house. House, if one took the liberty to call Shivakumar's abode by the side of the busy, glittering commercial road on the footpath as a house. House was for him and his family as it gave the comfort of familiarity and belonging in this large unknown city. The same comfort that everyone feels going back to their homes. Maybe the same comfort that immigrants feel when they visit their native land. The comfort that dogs feel in their lanes or birds in their nests. The corner on the pavement had the security of a tall wall at the back and an electrical panel on one side, giving them a perfect and private corner. The large tree next to the electrical panel gave enough shelter during the day. A jute sack in the corner next to the electrical panel held most of their belongings. A few feet away, three bricks arranged like a tripod formed their kitchen. At night, the area between the electrical panel and the kitchen would be transformed into a sleeping area with bedsheets spread on the pavement and a blanket to cover them if it got cold at night. The lamp post provided free light. They certainly had a few luxuries that others who lived in concrete boxes did not have. He and his family could sleep peacefully under the night sky without a drop of sweat, even on the hottest nights of the summer, even when there was a power cut.

Shivkumar passed the boys on the footpath without noticing, as if searching for something. They were busy looking down at the ground as they walked slowly along the busy street.

Shivkumar reached home excitedly and parked his bicycle, his priciest possession, along the wall and locked it with a chain and lock to the lamppost. His wife, Parvati, was preparing for dinner. Dried wood twigs that she had searched and collected throughout the day were burning in the brick tripod. An iron flat pan (tawa) rested on the tripod. Parvati meticulously flattened the wet jowar dough into flatbread or bhakri (Indian bread) and laid them on the tawa to cook. Shivkumar, all excited, looked for his son around the house and asked, "Where is Ghanu?"

"He must be playing with his friends down the footpath along the garden fence."

Leaving the kids alone, out of sight on a busy road, would be considered bad parenting. People watching kids playing alone on streets from their rolled-up car windows would think parents of these kids cared less for their kids or that these poor street people have so many kids that they care less for each one of them. Kidnapping, getting lost, or an accident on the street could be the top risks on their minds. Not for Shivkumar, Parvati, and many like them who shared a similar life. Maybe because that busy street and stretch of footpath was like their backyard. They lived there. Maybe they were ignorant of the perceived risks that the financially more fortunate ones felt. But for Shivakumar and Parvati, their son was as valuable to them as the judgmental parents in the car felt about theirs. Shivkumar sat down next to Parvati narrating how good his day was and that he had a good earning.

"Tomorrow is his birthday. We can take him to the pizza place and treat him to a large pizza that he has been longing for for so long."

"Do we have enough money?"

"Today was good. There was a kind man who gave me some extra work. He wanted his car tires changed. He even taught me how to do it and also paid handsomely. God bless him. It will be enough to buy a soft drink and a cake too."

Parvati was elated.

"God bless him." After a thoughtful pause, she continued, "What do you mean he taught you?"

"I had never changed car tires. He taught me and made me do it."

Saying this, Shivakumar reached into his pocket for the money. The money was missing, and Shivakumar panicked. He got up and checked his shirt pocket and then his pants pockets. He felt his pockets from outside for money, and he pulled out his pockets inside out, checking his shirt and pants again and again in panic. The money was nowhere to be found.

"I had it right here," he said, pointing to his pants pocket."

"I think I dropped it on the road on my way back."

Disheartened and dejected, he sat back down next to Parvati, tears welling out of his eyes. His small dream of fulfilling his son's small wish was crushed. Just then, he saw Ghanu coming back home from another end of the footpath. He wiped his eyes and controlled his emotions. He did not want to let Ghanu know about the hopes and disappointments of the past few minutes. Ghanu appeared more cheerful today with a bounce in his walk. He was carrying something in his hand. As Ghanu approached, he handed a box to Shivakumar.

"Dad, I got you a gift." Ghanu looked at Shivakumar's face with a sparkle in his eyes, expecting to see a smile, love, and happiness for his gift. Shivakumar opened the box. It was a wristwatch. Shivakumar, getting angry, said, "Where did you get the money for this, and why did you get the watch?" Ghanu could not understand the reason for his father's sudden anger instead of joy.

"Pappa, I got you a watch because you come late from work every day after I fall asleep. I don't get to meet you. You can use this watch so that you don't get late." Ghanu had expressions of concern and love on his face for a moment. Ghanu continued.

"I bought it using the money I found lying on the road there. Somebody must have dropped it."

Listening to this, Shivakumar held Ghanu close to his chest and did not leave him for minutes, tears rolling down his cheek.

"I will, son. I will use this watch and come home early."

Innocent Heart

She stood there amidst a hundred-odd people staring at her, crying, her world crumbling down around her.

It started a few days ago, the pestering, to do it against her will. She was clear in her mind. Everyone like her is usually very clear in their minds on what they want and what they don't. She was clear too. She did not want to get involved. They did everything to make her agree. There were promises made, then came the bribery, followed by emotional blackmail and eventually threats. But she was too determined on what she wanted, or rather she did not want, to falter to such efforts.

The night before, she was pestered again by him to perform. She was firm and confident, without any fear. She refused to give in to his pestering and declined his offer. She then hugged him and slept in his arms. He was her world; she loved him dearly. She loved him more than anyone else of the few people she had known in her little life. She had full faith in him, and she believed he was the best man there was and that he would never force her into anything that she did not like or anything that would make her cry. He has always been there for her, and she thought he would always be there to save her when she called for him in times of trouble, in times of need, in times of pain. But her trust was about to be broken.

She was too pure at heart to understand the crooked ways of this world. Before she could understand the game, she was asked to accompany him to where she was called upon. But she was clear she would not do it. She trusted him too much to suspect any wrongdoing. All along the way, she kept talking to him about her thoughts, aspirations, dreams, even the pettiest things that she felt, not suspecting once what was going to ensue. He listened to her intently, entertaining her, engaging her as he drove her to the destination. He loved her too.

When they arrived, a lady took her away to a different room. She was a naive soul. She did not realize the game. The malice of the world had not touched her. She still had virtues like trusting people and living in the moment. In the room, she got lost in the moment, getting busy chatting with others like her in that room.

Then the moment came. Their class teacher called upon all the kids sitting in the room to line up. It was time. Fear gripped her, but she had no option but to stand in the queue. In moments, the queue started moving forward out of the classroom toward the hall where the annual day event was being held. As she walked into the corridor overlooking the hall, fear gripped her. Her kindergarten classroom was supposed to perform a dance number in front of a hundred-odd audience, mainly parents and some grandparents.

The kids were lined up on the stage in straight lines facing the audience. She was moved to her position holding her hand by her teacher. The music started and with every drumbeat, kids started performing the steps taught to them over the past few weeks. She felt forced into something she never wanted to do. She froze. She couldn't move her limbs, or rather, she did not want to. She was scared. She started looking for the man of her life, her dad. He was there in the crowd, trying to encourage her and cheer her up. She couldn't find him.

The first part of the dance was completed, and the teacher signaled the kids to sit down for the remaining part of the performance. All the kids followed the command and sat down. There she stood in the middle of the stage, alone, helpless, with the crowd staring. She felt everyone was laughing at her. She broke into tears. Tears rolled down her cheeks as she continued looking for her father. Not able to locate him in the crowd for a while, she gave up. She went blank. She had no thoughts in her mind anymore; she only wanted to get out of that situation. With blurred vision due to tear-filled eyes, gasping for breath from crying continuously, she stood there alone, waiting. Minutes felt like centuries. Finally, to her relief, the song ended, and she was taken back to her classroom.

As the event ended and her dad received her outside her classroom, she broke into tears and hugged her dad tightly. She was having mixed feelings of relief and anger. She expressed her anger by punching him a few times on his shoulders with her delicate hands as he picked her up.

Moments passed. In the comforting embrace of her dad, resting her head on his shoulders, it was all forgotten and forgiven at that moment. Natalie returned to her happy self. With a twinkle in her eyes, a smile on her face, and chatter in her mouth, Natalie jumped and skipped holding Bernhard's hand as they walked back to the car for a drive back home.

Like all kids, Young Natalie still embraced the quality of forgive and forget. A quality that is so simple yet has the power to solve the world's smallest and biggest problems. For Natalie, with time and exposure to a more complex world, this golden trait would be forgotten. It would be replaced by more principled and idealistic expectations from herself and everyone around her.

Fisherman's Secret

Baban was desperately walking through the chest-deep water.

Sea was the home turf for Baban. He was born and brought up in the quintessential little hamlet in the coastal region of western India called Konkan. The Konkan coast is lined with numerous such little hamlets, which until recently were hidden from the world until they caught the eye of the well-to-do urban Indian. Tourism flourished. Locals opened up their homes for homestays, and city dwellers flocked to Konkan in bulk to enjoy the sand, sea, nature, and local food. Typically, homes in Konkan are surrounded by big coconut and supari plantations and the sea beyond, a stone's throw away, making it an idyllic location. Baban was not fortunate enough to take advantage of the tourism boom. He had a small hut and a small backyard with mango trees in a small fishing hamlet. His property was not good enough to let out for homestays.

In the chest-deep water, Baban spread his net again and waited for a while before gathering it back. Nothing. As Baban made a few more unsuccessful attempts at catching the fish, he got worried. He made one last desperate attempt as he realized taking home nothing would push him into an ordeal that would drag on for days; rather, it would stick with him for life. He prayed to God as he waited with the fishing net spread. After a few minutes, he slowly started gathering the net. He saw one small fish the size of half his palm caught in the net. It was barely anything. He at least needed one kilogram of it. Dejected, he removed the fish from the net and threw it back into the water. He was literally scared of what was to come if he did not take the fish home by noon.

Baban was a simple man. He was a man with few needs and even fewer means. Living in a fishing village without a boat of his own, he worked as the next best thing possible—a fisherman's helper. He would go deep-sea fishing with fishermen as their helper. The wage was decent, and a few free fishes out of the fresh catch for home was a bonus. He was a contented man.

Having dinner at seven in the evening, resting for a couple of hours, and then leaving for the night's work in the deep sea. That was his routine four days a week. He returned at dawn, bathed, and slept to wake up for lunch in the afternoon.

At the sea, Baban gave up after his last desperate attempt. He gathered his net and started walking back toward the shore from the chest-deep water. As he walked back, he wondered what options he had to take the fish home. Buying from the town market nearby was an option, provided he had the money to buy it. He had none. Baban cursed himself for not going to the sea the previous night. He could have had the money. Even better, he wouldn't have needed the money owing to the fresh catch that he could have carried home.

Baban was a lazy man, and if it weren't for his wife, he would not have worked at all. For the last three weeks, Baban's wife had traveled to her parents' place for her cousin's wedding. With his wife gone and no one there to push him for work, Baban stopped going to work as a fisherman's helper. Baban started with the excuse of a family emergency. That was followed by an excuse of not being well. No one likes an unreliable worker. By the end of two weeks, his recruiters stopped inquiring about Baban and recruited some other helper. Baban cared less. Baban spent his days lazing around at home. However, the drawback of all this was that Baban spent all the money he had on food and drink in a three-week time.

Baban dragged his feet on the beach sand as he walked toward his house. His mind raced, thinking about his options to get out of this situation he had lazed himself into. He asked the time from a vacationer enjoying the beach. It was two more hours before his wife returned. His wife's sister was accompanying her to stay with them for a day before she traveled further to her home. So it was all the more important to do as his wife had instructed him, to get the fish for lunch. She wanted to treat her sister with good food and make sure she had a good time. It was more than that. There was a little sibling rivalry going on there. It's always there between sisters. Showing off to her sister that she was doing well in life was important to Mala. Also, Mala wanted to outdo her sister in taking care of her, as compared to when Mala visited her. In any case, the wife's relatives are the most important people, and his falling short on any front in taking care of the relatives will not go well with Mala. That made Baban nervous.

Baban thought of visiting the fishing dock to request some fish from the day's catch. It was too late for that. But he was desperate and hence decided to give it a try. Typically, the fishermen return from the deep sea at dawn, and all the fish is segregated and bought by the distributor, carried away in trucks, and sold in the city within an hour. Some fish are bought by local traders to be sold in the nearby town market. Local traders would have bought their fish from the fishermen and left for the market by this time. When Baban reached the fishing dock, there was no one except one of his old employers, Machindra, a local big shot. He owned three boats. He had some fresh fish he had kept aside to carry home. Baban pleaded with Machindra to give him the fish. Had it not been for Baban's laziness, Machindra would have given his fish to Baban. His request was denied owing to Baban's carelessness and not showing up for work.

The previous afternoon, Mala had called Baban to inform him that she was coming back home along with her sister the next day. Mala had instructed him to get fresh fish for lunch. Baban knew this was important to her, so he wanted to make it happen, not only because he loved Mala so dearly but also because he was scared of the wrath she would bring upon him if he failed her. Mala was a loving wife, but knowing the lazy ways of her husband, she had to become a taskmaster at times. He would have a tough time facing Mala for days if he did not get the fish. After the call with Mala to earn money and get the fish, he went and talked to Machindra, whom Baban had ditched for the past three weeks. Unwillingly, after a lot of pleading, Machindra took him back to work. Happy with his triumph, Baban went back home, promising the fisherman to be at the boat that evening. Unfortunately, he didn't. Baban had dozed off only to wake up 30 minutes after the boat had left. Baban rushed to the fishing dock to find that all the boats had left.

It had been only two years since they got married. Baban and Mala were young. Mala was 23 when she got married. Baban wasn't too old himself. He was 25. Baban was a lone soul. His father had passed away in a mishap during a storm when he was 21. His mother died soon after due to illness. That left him alone and aimless in this world. Time passed, but nothing motivated Baban. He spent days doing nothing. He did not work and did not earn. He had few relatives in nearby villages, including his aunts and uncles, who took care of him. One in particular, Aunt Kaveri, his mother's sister. Truly cared for him. Over time, she successfully guided him in starting to work and get on with his life.

As time passed, Aunt Kaveri felt Baban needed a companion and an anchor in life in the form of a wife; otherwise, he would waste his life doing nothing. Aunt Kaveri, through her friends and relatives, spread the word about a young eligible bachelor in their community. Soon, she heard back from a few prospective matches. Baban did not have parents alive, and that worked in his favor in the marriage market. Prospective brides' parents liked a match where there are no in-laws to meddle. Aunt Kaveri and Baban visited and met several of these prospective brides. Baban was young, and he had high expectations of the girl he wanted to marry. Baban wanted his bride to be pretty and from a well-to-do family. He declined a few proposals after the first meeting owing to his high expectations. There were a few cases where the girls' parents rejected Baban due to his low income. Mala's parents were one of them. Baban and Aunt Kaveri had visited Mala's house to meet her. Mala was fair and pretty. Baban fell in love with her the first time he met her at her house. Baban and Aunt Kaveri had visited them. Baban was disappointed when he heard about the rejection.

Days passed, but he couldn't get Mala out of his mind. One morning, Baban decided to meet Mala on the spur of the moment. Baban shaved, showered, put on the best clothes he had, and left for Mala's place. It was a scenic coastal route winding through small hills. However, Baban was lost in his dreams about Mala to notice the natural beauty.

Baban was decently handsome, but there was nothing about Baban that stuck in Mala's mind or heart. Mala had not given a second thought to her parents rejecting Baban. Baban waited for two hours outside Mala's house, waiting for her to leave the house. He knew that he would not be welcomed at her house. Baban followed Mala and approached her when they reached a secluded stretch of road far from her home. It took Mala a moment to identify Baban. Baban tried to sound polite and sincere when he expressed his liking toward Mala and his wish to marry her. This was sudden, unexpected, and something new for Mala. It made her angry. She warned Baban not to trouble her, or else she would complain about him to her parents. Baban pleaded with her to give it a thought and left.

Baban met Mala again a few days later and expressed his wish to her once more. Mala's response was the same. Mala never complained about this to her parents. Whether it was fear of getting scolded for meeting Baban or unknowingly she was inclined to protect someone who expressed his liking toward her, she could never explain. Baban met Mala a few more times. Mala found his perseverance endearing. With every meeting, Mala found her anger melting away. The feeling of being liked by someone is blissful and infectious. Before Mala could realize it, she started liking Baban as well. It made her angry, and she unsuccessfully tried to fight the emotions that she was feeling for Baban. She realized she had started hoping Baban would be waiting to meet her every time she stepped out of her house. Eventually, their phone numbers were exchanged, and interaction increased. A couple of months passed, and they were deeply in love and wanted to get married.

It took a lot of convincing from everyone before Mala's father agreed to their marriage. Baban even committed to working hard and owning his own boat. And that is history. Two years down, Baban wasn't even close to buying a motorcycle, let alone a boat. Baban meant well, and he wanted to provide the best of the world for Mala, but his laziness did not help the cause. Mala meant well, too, and wanted the best for both of them.

With no catch from the sea and being shooed away by Machindra, Baban had started to panic. His mind was racing for a solution as he paced back from the docks toward his home. He dreaded facing Mala without having the fish. It was evident that buying fish from the nearby town market was the only option. There was no fish market in the village. Everyone was either a fisherman or their helper. They all carried fresh catch home. For them, buying fish was stupid, and Baban had lazed himself in a situation where he was forced to do that stupidity. The sad part was that he did not have money even though he wished to do that stupidity.

So his focus shifted from getting fish to getting money for the fish. Baban had earned an ill reputation as a lazy, unreliable chap through his deeds. Baban thought of borrowing money from the neighbors. But knowing about his reputation, he realized they would not lend him any money. Even if they did, neighbors would talk, and Mala would know about this, which would be a bigger problem. As Baban walked back, he thought of everyone who could possibly lend him money. Baban could trace back how the information of him borrowing money would flow back to Mala in each of the cases. Momentarily, Baban felt proud of his deduction skills, but to no avail. His problem at hand was still there as it was. Baban cursed himself for being lazy and steering himself into the trouble he was in currently.

Fresh from all the convincing and commitments, Baban ventured into their married life with a lot of rigor and dedication to fulfill his promises. Mala was also very loving and supportive of Baban. But as they say, 'old habits die hard ', Baban slowly slipped into lethargy and slowed down. He would find excuses to avoid work. Mala was supportive initially, believing that Baban's excuses were genuine. But soon, she realized Baban's excuses were just to get out of work. Mala couldn't sit and watch Baban lazing his life, rather their life into poverty. She knew Baban was a good man, and he cared for her. She felt it was up to her to keep Baban on track. Mala decided to run a tight ship. Mala tendered, loved, and cared for Baban with all her heart and soul. But when it came to Baban's laziness, she became a taskmaster. Baban was aware of his shortcomings and knew

Mala did it for his own good and for their better future. With time Mala got so good at keeping Baban on track that she commanded fear in Baban's heart for not following Mala's instructions. The current fear of not getting the fish for Mala's sister came from this legacy of running a tight ship by Mala.

Sun was approaching high in the sky as Baban briskly walked toward his house, sweating profusely out of heat and panic. As his mind started drifting toward excuses, he could present Mala for not getting fish, Baban corrected the course of his thinking. Baban knew that no excuse could exonerate him from this crime, and he wouldn't hear the end of it for life from Mala for this crime. Baban dreaded it. He realized he had to find a way out. Right then, a ray of brilliance struck him. Baban remembered a conversation he had with Mala. That monsoon night, Baban was at home as rain was pouring, and the fishermen were not going to the sea that night. The villagers had retired inside their houses early. The streets were pitch dark due to power cuts. Power cuts were frequent during the rains in their village. Dim candles and lanterns lit the homes. Most could not afford the emergency power backup. It was an accepted way of life even for those who could afford it when there was a power cut. Mala finished her chores after dinner and went to the inner room. Baban lay there quietly in the dim light of the lantern. She adjusted the flame to decrease the light further. Usually cheerful and talkative, Baban was quiet the whole evening. Mala knew something was bothering him. Mala knew Baban would tell her what was troubling him when he was ready. Mala sat close to Baban's head quietly and started moving her fingers through Baban's hair as rain poured outside. Mala could see Baban's worried face in the dim lantern light. After a while, Baban broke his silence. Baban expressed that he was feeling sad and worried about their future. It has been more than a year since he resolved to take his future seriously and save money to own a boat. Baban had realized that he had not been able to save much during the past year. Mala knew that Baban had worked hard voluntarily for the first few months, and Mala had made him focus on the goal after an interim lull due to his laziness. Mala continued to move her fingers as she heard Baban speak. Baban had tears in his eyes, and Mala could hear his voice well up as he expressed how much he loved Mala and he wanted the best for her. He expressed his regret for not being able to provide for her enough.

There are moments when deep-rooted pains, grief, and insecurities surface in everyone's life. It's in the moment, and probably the darkness and quiet of the night bring out the grief. It was such a moment for Baban. The wet thunderstorm was doing no good. These moments pass, and most people are resilient enough to survive and continue to go about their lives normally, burying back such grief deep somewhere in the psyche.

After a while, Baban stopped speaking. The moment had passed for him. Mala sat there silently. Baban's moment of fear and insecurity was adorable for Mala because it was for their future and out of his deep love for her. It was true, it was honest, it was straight from his heart. Mala felt immense love for Baban. She wanted him to feel better. Mala took his head in her lap. Mala said, trying to bring some cheerfulness in her voice, "You are such an adorable stupid baby of mine. We will make it happen. It may take a couple of years more than we planned for, but we will make it happen".

Mala continued, "And there is some money I..." before stopping abruptly. Mala did not want to reveal the money she was secretly saving for their future.

The line that Mala did not complete echoed in Baban's mind. Baban was elated. He started rushing toward his home in anticipation that there was a stash of money hidden somewhere inside his house that would save him from a lifetime of taunting. As Baban paced back, his chappals stitches came off. Baban didn't care as he limped back home, dragging his foot along the ground so that his chappals did not come off. Baban reached home, drenched in sweat, and started looking for the money. It was 1.5 hours before Mala arrived with her sister and her family. Within that time, Baban needed to find money, rush to the nearby town market, and get the fish. Now that Baban had hope of finding money, he got very nervous about the time. He went straight to the cupboard to search for money but without success. Then he searched the drawer next to the bed, under the mattress, luggage trunk, and everywhere else in the house. There was no sign of the money. Tired and exhausted, he stood there in the middle of the house, taking a pause while breathing heavily. With no sign of money, what he dreaded seemed inevitable now. He knew it was not the end of the world, and he would survive it. But what Baban dreaded was the harsh, ruthless taunting that he would have to face once Mala's sister and her family left if he was not able to serve fish during their visit. It would not be forgotten for the rest of his life.

As Baban stood there comprehending the situation he was in, he noticed the kitchen steel containers, or dabba as they call it in the local language. There were around 15 dabbas of different sizes in the kitchen. Baban was clueless about what was stored in each of the dabbas. Baban started opening the dabbas one by one, checking for money. The world of the kitchen was unknown to Baban. He had never contributed to kitchen chores, ever. Mala did not expect that from Baban. As Baban opened dabbas one after another, he discovered which dabba had sugar, flour, and lentils. He did not care for that. All he cared for was the money. Still no sign of money. Next, Baban skipped a few and targeted the largest dabba on the rack. He tried to open the lid with his fingers without lifting the dabba. The lid was fastened tightly, and he could not open it. To apply better force, he lifted the dabba. It was a heavy one. He held the dabba close to his chest with his left hand and tried to open the lid with the fingers of his right hand. As Baban applied his full strength, the lid suddenly opened with force, and the dabba slipped out of his hand. Before he could recover, the dabba fell on the floor, and the rice in the dabba scattered across the floor. He saw a bunch of money in the middle of the kitchen floor scattered with rice.

Baban was able to clean up the kitchen and rush to the market to get the fish in time before Mala and her sister arrived. Baban also got the rice to refill the spilled rice.

Three months had passed since the dabba mishap, and Baban was able to earn and replenish the money in the rice dabba without Mala knowing about the missing money or the replenished rice. Mala knew her husband very well and sensed something was wrong. To this day, Baban is not able to look Mala in the eye when she asks him about the rice grains that she kept finding in nooks and crannies in her kitchen for months after she came back from her parents.

Happily Ever After

A debate was brewing in the living room of Revathi and Harpreet's home. The family was divided into two groups. One group led by Harpreet had Adi and Natalie in it. The other group was led by Revathi and comprised of Malini. Sameer was confused and wasn't able to make up his mind. To avoid an argument with Malini later, he leaned more on Revathi's side.

Natalie and Adi had visited Mumbai for the wedding reception that Revathi and Harpreet had planned. It was a big Punjabi-style reception that Harpreet wanted. Sameer and Malini had also accompanied Adi and Natalie to India.

"Adi and Natalie were better off without your meddling," Harpreet said.

"If it wasn't for me, my dear son would still be beating around the bush without committing," Revathi said.

Natalie laughed remembering that phase of their courtship. Adi felt embarrassed, knowing what Revathi was refering to.

"It would have taken time, but I would have proposed eventually," Adi defended himself.

"Ya, right," Malini replied sarcastically.

"No, you wouldn't have proposed. Not in a million years." Even Sameer did not believe that.

"What about the mess that got created between them due to your meddling?" Harpreet made a point.

"He was already in a mess by hiding I was his mother," Revathi replied.

"The mess was much smaller before the meddling. The Turkey and Germany visit from you, Amma, made Adi's mistake seem huge at that time. I felt, I was deceived and cheated by him. That, too, for no fault of Adi in it." Natalie tried to defend her poor husband who was getting massacred by Revathi in the debate.

"Aww, so cute. My dear daughter-in-law defending my stupid son." Revathi was unrelenting in pulling Adi.

The debate went on without any conclusion. They eventually had to agree to disagree.

It had been months since Adi and Natalie had returned to Berlin from their India visit. Revathi and Harpreet were sitting in front of the TV, having their morning coffee. Natalie, now their daughter-in-law, was presenting the world news on DE Media. The show went into a commercial break. Revathi showed up on the TV screen. DE Media was playing various snippets of Natalie's documentary; Revathi's interview was one of them. The snippet of Natalie and

Revathi's interview when they first met in Turkey played on TV.

"What is one relationship tip that you would give the world?"

"People's personalities are influenced by the neural wiring they are born with and their life experiences. Personalities differ at several levels, which makes relationships challenging. I am not limiting this to romantic relationships only. Whether it is between spouses, siblings, friends, or parents and children. Being accommodating of others' perspectives rather than expecting from others your own definition of perfection is the key to making relationships easier and more enjoyable."

The documentary snippet ended, and a different commercial came on the TV.

"Wow. So true. Impressive," Harpreet exclaimed.

"I am married to the prettiest and the smartest woman there is," Harpreet added. Revathi almost blushed at Harpreet's flattery.

The new show resumed, and Natalie was back on screen, live.

"There is a different glow on Natalie's face today. Do you see it? She looks so happy."

"Don't start this again, please. They are already married. What is it now?"

"When I had a video call with Adi yesterday, he seemed a little lost and self-absorbed, as if worried about something."

Revathi paused and thought for a while before continuing with a big smile.

"I know what it is."

"What?" Harpreet asked curiously.

"Natalie is pregnant."

Harpreet trusted Revathi's observation. He did not need any proof this time.

END